THE
GAMEKEEPER'S
SON

THE
GAMEKEEPER'S
SON

RON STEWART

To order additional copies of this book, contact:
Xlibris
1-888-795-4274
www.Xlibris.com
Orders@Xlibris.com
713337

CONTENTS

ABOUT THE SKETCH ARTIST

I was having some difficulty finding a suitable artist to create
a small sketch for each story depicting the contents. They
all seemed so amateurish and not worthy of a place in my
book. In desperation I called a good friend of mine who was
president of the local sketch club. His response was that he was
too busy to commit himself to the task but knew of a young
woman Sandra Orrins in the club who was very good.

We met at the next sketchers meeting when she brought some
samples of her work. I could not believe the quality and accuracy
of the samples, every one perfect. After a meeting the following
week Sandra agreed to take on the job, I was over joyed.
Not only an excellent artist, Sandra also runs a smallholding with her
husband including all kinds of animals and fowl and a large garden.
Sandra is also credited with being the coauthor of wonderful cook book,
her sketches and some of her own receipts. This book is a must have

PREFACE

It has been brought to my attention that not everyone knows what a gamekeeper really is, in fact, while going over some thoughts on the subject before I started writing, I now realize how complex and difficult this task is going to be.

He is hired by the Laird, the owner of an ESTATE to protect all the game from predators and poachers {people who take game illegally}. An estate may consist of hundreds of square miles and a few dozen farms also owned by the laird and leased to individual farmers. In the case of very large estates such as this it would be necessary for him to hire as many as six gamekeepers each with his own section or {beat} to look after. In addition to a to a small wage he would also have the use of a house owned by the estate with firewood, coal, milk and oatmeal included, for as long as he remained in the employment of the laird.

A gamekeepers day would start at daybreak and end at dusk seven days a week but he did have some time to himself during the day when all his work was taken care of. When he was not out setting or checking his traps or snares for rabbits he would be in his workshop repairing them. He had to maintain about forty traps and twice as many snares. He made all the snares from scratch including the wooden pegs. He made all his bolt nets too. These were about three feet square with a draw string woven in and out round the perimeter to which was attached a peg. He usually made them in the long winter evenings, sitting by the fire and listening to the radio.

He was also required to protect the nests of game birds such as Partridge, Pheasant and Grouse from predators, the worst offender being the "hooded crow" a very wily bird that would nest in the tall pine trees. The gamekeeper would build a hide close to the nest and sit and wait sometimes for hours until the crow returned and he could shoot it. Weasels and badgers also created havoc on the birds' nests and had to be controlled too.

Poachers were always a problem. When he would find some strange traps or snares on his rounds he would leave them intact and find a secluded spot nearby and wait until the poacher returned and apprehend him. His traps e.t.c. would be confiscated and sent on his way with a swift kick on the posterior and the threat of death should he ever be caught there again. The police were seldom involved.

The gamekeeper was well respected in the community and was classed with the doctor, minister, schoolteacher and policeman and was regarded as one of the main sources of information in rural areas since there were no telephones and few folks had radio. We had a radio[a Christmas gift from the Laird] so he was much saught after for information regarding the progress of the war with the Germans.

Anyone could depend on him for comfort or advice in any situation and he was always a willing giver.

THE OWL

The collecting of sheep's wool was a never-ending chore. My father would constantly remind me, "If you have nothing to do, get wool." He used it to stuff pillows for his beehives to help keep them warm in winter. I had been round the sheep fences so often I now had to go farther afield to find a new supply.

It was on one of these foraging missions that I came upon a dead sheep in an advanced state of decay. Although the smell was a little overpowering, I had hit the jackpot as far as wool was concerned. It came free from the carcass in big handfuls, so in no time I had filled the burlap sack.

As I made my way home, a spring in my step and humming a tune to match, I spotted a large bird sitting on a fence post directly in my path not twenty feet away. I slowly lowered the bag of wool to the ground and quietly made my way toward it. It was an owl. I had never seen an owl this close before. In fact, I had seen very few owls at all.

It made no attempt to escape as I cautiously approached. We now looked each other straight in the eye. What a magnificent bird!

Slowly I raised my right hand. Would it allow me to touch it?

As my hand came level with its perch, I got the shock of my life when it just walked onto my hand. It didn't leap, jump or flutter, just one foot after the other onto my hand, closing its talons on my pointing finger.

The pressure of its grip surprised me, to the extent that I realized getting it off might present a problem. Maybe it would fly away if I lifted my hand quickly? No, it only dug its claws in deeper to resist any attempt to get rid of it.

I picked up the bag of wool with my free hand and headed for home again, the owl firmly attached to my hand regardless of all the motions I was making.

I had only gone a hundred yards or so when the pain in my hand became unbearable. Something had to be done. A thought came to me — if it worked before, it might work again. I brought my hand with the owl over to my left shoulder then, wonder of wonders, it again walked slowly from my hand onto my shoulder, and there he stayed all the way home.

As I entered our backyard, the bird flew from my shoulder onto the firewood rack, a contraption designed by Dad (two uprights and a cross bar some eight feet off the ground) to lean the small firewood trees against.

Breaking the news of my newfound friend had to wait until supper time. Even then no one seemed to care very much. Dad said, "That thing'll be gone afore morning."

I checked on it several times during the evening. Its eyes would follow me everywhere I went.

Early the following morning I rushed out to see how true Dad's prediction was. He was wrong. There sat the owl on his lofty perch and, as I approached the firewood rack, there came another surprise. It glided gracefully from its post onto my left shoulder, and there it stayed as I walked around. I wondered if it would stay there when I had to go indoors. The moment I reached the door the bird was gone, however, back to his perch. It was time to catch the bus to school anyway.

Most days I would walk the couple of miles home from school. Otherwise I would have to wait another hour for the bus. Two of my classmates lived on the same route; thus we always had company.

No time was wasted getting home that night. As soon as I was in view of the wood rack, the owl took off in my direction. This time it didn't land on my shoulder, but landed at my feet and walked with me the rest of the way home, where it returned to its favorite spot on the wood rack.

As every other night, I changed into working clothes before walking the half-mile to the farm to get the milk. I grabbed the pails and set off. I had a pleasant fright when the owl landed on my shoulder (always the right one). It stayed there for a little while, then dropped to the ground and waddled alongside of me the rest of the way. On reaching the farm it would find a high perch and wait for me to appear for the return trip, which it made either by riding on my shoulder or walking beside me.

This daily routine never changed for weeks to come. The strange part of our relationship was, there was no training involved. I never offered food to the bird. It was always right there as if waiting for me, and it would never go near any other people.

On the weekends when my older sister came home, she would lend me her bicycle to go for the milk. As usual, the owl would land on my shoulder but, when I was mobile on the bicycle, it would alight on the handlebars and go slowly up and down with outstretched wings—a beautiful sight that gave me the opportunity to closely examine the unique structure of the bird in flight.

When the bird first found me in early spring it was quite large, but then, by midsummer, it had almost doubled its size

At this time we had an old black Lab, not a working dog, just a pet that lay around the place begging to be walked. There was no love lost between the owl and the Lab. I can recall one hot sultry afternoon when the old dog was lying baking in the sun. The flies were bothering him and he was already in a disgruntled mood.

Mr. Owl from his lookout saw the opportunity for some devilment here. He swooped down and landed about ten feet from the dog. Ever so slowly, one step at a time, he crept up on the poor sleeping brute, slowly lifted one leg in the air, then swiftly clamped it down on the dog's tail.

A loud yelp broke the serenity of the day, followed by a large cloud of dust as the Lab gained traction in hot pursuit of the fleeing bird.

From where I stood, I could see this owl was no dummy. It headed for the woods at ground level, fluttering its wings as if it was wounded, weaving in and out of the trees only a few feet ahead of the dog's snapping jaws. When the owl thought the dog had had enough, he soared back to the safety of the woodpile.

This was just one such incident I witnessed. There were others, too, and always instigated by the owl.

One hot sunny afternoon my parents had visitors—some aunt and uncle and two or three of their offspring. I can't recall exactly who they were. I do remember they were all very fat. The big fat lady was seated in a chair next to the open window with her arm resting on the windowsill, when I saw my owl land on the sill outside not inches from her hand.

The flight of an owl is so quiet. I had read this, but it was not until I had met my owl that I could fully grasp how quiet they really are.

The owl had been there for a good five minutes before it was noticed by the fat lady, who gave out this ear-piercing scream, frightening the wits out of my owl and everyone else in the room. It took some time to console the party. Mam rushed to make a cup of tea, while Dad tried to reassure them with the promise that that very night it would fall before his twelve-gauge.

My father never did carry out that threat, of course.

That evening, after the guests had all left, he was helping Mam clean up. "Fit a fleg yer owl gied that wifie," he said, as he retreated laughing into the kitchen with a handful of dishes.

I could fill a book with the other stories of my owl, but we must move on.

Come the time of year when the trees lose their leaves and we see the first snowflakes, my owl spent less and less time at our house. I remember going out one morning—no owl. He was there when I came home from school, but from then on his absences became more frequent until one day he never did return.

Right up until the end, he never showed any less affection for me.

My father was right.

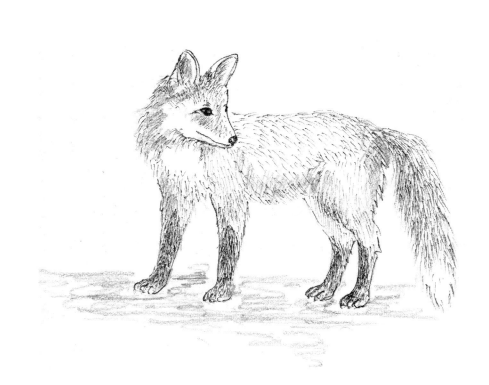

THE FOX

It was probably the year 1947, and I was going to school in Rothes. We lived in the Little Haugh Cottages in the glen of Rothes at this time, a beautiful setting of fields and heather-covered hills. The farm next door was owned by a sheep farmer, Mr. Shaw (everyone referred to him as "Sheepy Shaw").

Amongst my father's many interests and hobbies was beekeeping. He had kept bees all his life and made his own hives, including the inner parts that held the wax foundations for the honeycombs. He made the straw hives, called "skeps," by the dozen. He sold some locally, but the bulk of them were orders from a large bee supply company called Steel and Broddy. When the honey was harvested, the bees had to be given food of some kind to tide them through the winter. This was usually a weak sugar and water solution.

During the war with the Jerrys from 1939 to 1945, sugar was a scarce commodity indeed, but if you kept bees you would be allowed extra coupons to buy sugar for every live hive you owned. (The powers that be would send out inspectors from time to time to assure the hives you claimed had bees in them.) Dad, being the wheeler-dealer that he was, saw an opportunity to make some extra money here.

In his daily routine checking his traps or snares, he came upon a number of birch trees that had been recently scored with a knife and so set up that the juice dripped into a bottle tied to the tree. Curiosity got the better of him, so he waited in hiding until another beekeeper known to him appeared with a bucket and emptied all the bottles into it. "Foo wid Ton Gardine be collecting birk joos noo?" he mused as he made his way home.

Next day, after he had checked his tackle (traps, snares, etc.), he decided to call on Tony Gardine with some lame excuse regarding beekeeping that he was sure Tony could answer. Tony showed little or no expression as he listened to my father's plea for help in the matter, but inside he was bubbling with pride since the shoe was usually on the other foot. He poured out all kinds of information whether requested or not until in desperation my father had to bring up the subject that Tony, until now, had so skillfully avoided.

"Fits at stuff yer feedin' em noo, Ton?" enquired my father, knowing full well what it was and recognizing the now-empty bucket. "Oh! I canna tell ye at, Geordie. Ye see, it's a secret mixture handed doon fae gineration tae gineration." Dad acknowledged Tony's situation and bid him a hearty cheerio.

And so it was that my younger sister Mairi and I were equipped with bottles, string and knives, and a brief instruction on how to tap the birch trees. We had to tend the trees twice a day, before and after school. Since my father had found an alternate for sugar, the black market was hungry for his newfound product.

Not only do bees need food to see them through the winter, warmth is also a must. My father, with the help of my mother, made quilts or cushion-type things that fitted into the inside of the lid of the hive to help stop any heat from escaping. They worked very well, to the extent that I was recruited to search every fence for miles around and collect the sheep's wool that was hung up on the barbed wire. Wool was perfect for stuffing the cushions.

One evening after school as I was doing my rounds of the fences, on cresting a slight rise I noticed I was not the only one collecting wool. A fox, not fifty yards away, unaware of my presence, was also collecting wool. Judging by the amount he had in his mouth, he must have been at it for quite some time. I watched him for another fifteen minutes and saw him head for the burn (creek).

There was a small pool there where I often went fishing. I thought he might be going for a drink. No. He turned his rear end to the water and ever so slowly backed into it. The tuft of wool still in his mouth, he continued to slide slowly into the water until only his snout and the tuft of wool remained above water.

This whole process must have taken at least fifteen to twenty minutes.

Before my very eyes the fox let go of the lump of wool and submerged …
and disappeared. The tuft of wool just floated away downstream.

At the dinner table that night I had a story to tell, but I had to wait my
turn. The dinner table was not only a place to eat, it was where everyone
shared their experiences, stories, thoughts and grievances. Dad would
tell of his day first, followed by the oldest to the youngest. I will never
understand why my mother was always last.

On this particular evening when it came to my turn, I went through
my entire experience with the fox in great detail and with gestures.
Everyone listened with apparent interest, and when I finished I prepared
myself for the avalanche of questions and suggestions that were bound to
follow—when my father took the wind out of my sails with this statement.

"Och! I've seen that mair than ance. The beastie wis jist gittin' rid o'
ees flees."*

*As the fox slowly backed into the water, the fleas would travel up its body
to its head and finally onto the wool.

MANEUVERS

When we came home from school, the first order of the day for my sister and me was to walk the mile or so to the farm of Pittensair with two half-gallon cans and collect the milk. We were never in a hurry. We could dawdle along, maybe try to catch a rabbit in the bushes along the fence. If we heard a train coming we would run to the stone railway bridge and watch it pass under, spewing clouds of black smoke around us. In the summertime we were always barefoot, which could sometimes be a hazard if we took a shortcut through the clover-covered fields. Thousands of honey bees invested them, so getting stung was almost a certainty. The trick was to run at top speed, no stopping, to the opposite side. This always worked going there, but was not such a good idea for the return trip with two full cans of milk.

Winter time, with darkness approaching around 3:00 p.m., my older sister Cath would accompany one of us for the trip. The walk involved passing through the army camp where a sentry stood in a little box, rifle in hand, checking everyone who passed. There was never a problem during the hours of daylight. In fact, he would greet us warmly and chat as long as we stood there. Maybe it was the presence of Cath, now a pretty, young teenager.

Darkness brought a whole different situation, however. On approaching the sentry you would be challenged with the command, "HALT! WHO GOES THERE?" You were required to answer with, "Friend." To which he would reply, "Advance, friend, and be recognized." This was no game and was strictly enforced. If you didn't answer his first challenge, you would hear the bolt of his rifle being rammed back before he asked you a second time, and when you did advance to be recognized you faced a rifle leveled at your head.

Like anything else, one got used to it, even looked forward to it.

It was particularly challenging for my brothers coming home on leave from their units. They would get off the bus at the main road, then walk in through the camp. More than once my father was summoned to the guard room to clear up the situation.

Mock battles, or for a better name, maneuvers, were a daily occurrence. Even at night there was the crack of rifles, the boom of thunder-flashes (big firecrackers that simulated hand grenades) and phosphorus bombs that turned night into day.

One particular maneuver I recall involved two separate groups. One, with blackened faces to simulate the enemy, was transported out of the camp during the day. Their task was to infiltrate the camp unnoticed and blow up the petrol dumps, munitions, generators, etc. Of course, no real explosives would be used. A piece of chalk used to make a big cross would render the object "destroyed."

One officer had informed my father of the upcoming event, so he told us at breakfast that morning that he would pick up the milk himself that afternoon to avoid anyone going out during the operation.

That night the defending group was pretty sure they had captured all the black-faced invaders before they could do any damage. Surprise, surprise. The following morning found white crosses everywhere; even the door to headquarters had a cross on it.

That evening came a knock at the door. "Fa wid that be noo?" mused my father as he headed for the door. There stood a young mess boy in a spotless white jacket holding a pile of freshly laundered girl's clothes and two milk pails in his outstretched hands.

"Sir," says he, "I have been sent to return these and to inform you that your presence is requested in the officers' mess." Without waiting for an answer the young man took one step back, saluted smartly and was gone.

Dad laid the articles on the table, reached for his jacket and said to Mam (who was smiling at him with shared satisfaction), "I'll see ye in a wee whilie," then disappeared out the door.

"Fit were they dein we Cath's clais and the milk pails?" I queried.

"Niver you mind. Awa ye go tae yer bed."

LOCH-NA-BO

Of all the different places we lived from my childhood through my teens, the best of all was Loch-Na-Bo, seven miles from Elgin, one mile from Lhanbryde, in the county of Morayshire. The loch itself was maybe a mile long and half a mile wide, noted for its abundance of trout and surrounded on all sides by tall pine trees. It was all part of the estate belonging to the family of Innes, for whom my father worked as one of their several gamekeepers. The gamekeeper's cottage where we lived was situated next to the "big house," at one time a residence for one of the Innes brothers but then, like many other such dwellings, commandeered by the military as a headquarters. The surrounding acreage was converted into a huge army camp and training grounds. The loch served as an excellent place to practice bridge building and other water-related projects. There was never a day went by without the odd explosion and the rattle of gunfire, huge supply trucks and the small, tracked Bren gun carriers clattering everywhere. We were used to the noise and turmoil going on around us and didn't let it affect our daily routines very much.

This, you can well imagine, was the perfect heaven for an eight-year-boy like me. There were new happenings every day. My sister Mairi, two years my junior, was my constant companion in all my exploits since there were no other children for miles around. We attended Cranloch School together, a two-mile walk, summer and winter. There were twenty-five children in the two-room school, with three in my class, a headmaster and Miss Riddle the junior teacher.

In those days every child was issued a gas mask, which we had to carry to school. From time to time the teacher would shout, "GAS!" The last few to get their masks on would have to write "I am going to die" fifty or even one hundred times and present them to the teacher the next morning. It was not long before one realized the necessity for speed. Aside from these drills I cannot recollect ever having to use these masks in school, but my sister and I did have to use ours quite a few times coming through the camp on our way to and from school. In the event of gas being used (usually tear gas) in any of their frequent mock battles, an officer or NCO (noncommissioned officer) would be appointed to escort us the last three hundred yards home. Yes, the masks really did work, but not too many people had the occasion to prove it, as my sister and I did.

The officers' mess hall was directly opposite the back door of our cottage. Therefore, any leftover food would find its way into our house. In those days of such severe rationing, this food was a godsend, and what we didn't need I would take to school and pass it around to the neediest or trade for apples, eggs, milk and other farm products that were difficult for our family to get.

My most sought-after barter merchandise were the hundreds of empty brass bullet cases I had access to, mostly .303-caliber crimped blank ones, but on a quiet day I would sneak out to the range where I could pick up the proper empty .303 cases, also 9-millimeter from Sten guns, .45 caliber and the occasional .50 caliber (a real treasure).

Our family consisted of my mother, father, three older brothers, two older sisters, one younger sister, Mairi, and myself. At that time my three older brothers were in the army. Ian, the oldest, was in the Seaforth Highlanders. George, more often referred to as Dodd, was in the Gordon Highlanders and later transferred to the Royal Artillery. Robert (Bert) was moved around too, eventually ending up in The Green Howards. They all saw much conflict, and Ian was lost.

My two older sisters, Catherine and Lena (the eldest), worked as lumberjacks, or as we said, "worked in the woods." They peeled logs for telephone poles or pit props for the mines, or felled trees with double-handed crosscut saws. Hard work for a woman, you might think, but there were no men left to do the job; the men were all at war.

My father, a veteran of "the 14–18 war," as he called it, was too old for this one yet claimed, "I could still stop a bullet as good as the next one." He was kept busy full-time trying to keep ahead of the rabbit population and the poachers, who were usually Tinks (Gypsies).

Each gamekeeper on the estate had his own beat, or section, to look after, which could amount to quite a number of square miles. There would be a number of farms on each beat, all owned by the Laird—in this case, Major Ian Tenant. The farms were leased to individual farmers. I think the term of lease was something like a hundred years.

Now, the rabbits at this time were a big problem, destroying everything the farmer planted. The farmer would complain to the Laird, then the Laird would have to talk with the gamekeeper responsible for that area. When trapping or snaring, which were the usual methods of control, proved ineffective, other solutions had to be explored.

In that part of the world, rabbits live in burrows, holes in the ground. If the burrows are located in a sand bank, there could be literally hundreds of feet of tunnels, all interconnected, and just as many entrances and exits, making the rabbits almost impossible to trap.

This is where the bolt net comes in—a 36-inch-square of net with maybe an inch and a half mesh, a stout cord woven in and out around its perimeter with both ends of the cord attached to a peg to anchor it to the ground. The net is stretched over the entrance to the burrow and the peg is driven into the ground with the heel of your boot. You might have to set forty or fifty of these nets depending on the size of the warren.

So, you have set all your nets, filled your pipe, had your smoke. You are all ready for the action. You have brought along your two ferrets in the 8-x-8-x-14-inch box you made with the shoulder strap and the snap closure you've cycled from an old waterproof jacket. You lift a corner of a net and slip a ferret into the hole. Quickly, at the other side of the warren, you repeat the process. No sooner have you straightened your back when—*wump*!—a rabbit has exited at top speed, hitting the net and forcing it to close like a drawstring bag. You pounce on it, open the bag, grab the rabbit, snap its neck, throw it aside and proceed to reset the net. Before you get it reset another two nets have rabbits in them calling for your attention. You grab the nearest, snap the neck, dump the net, no time to reset, grab the third one, snap, a rabbit shoots out of the previous hole airborne to freedom.

And so the pandemonium continues for the next forty-five minutes. Well, you got more than 60 percent of them. You now realize this is more than a one-man job. In a short time the ferrets show themselves and are back in their box. That day's take was 34 rabbits, not bad for 60 percent.

If this had been done for the sport, this would have been one heck of a day, but to my father it was just another job that had to be done.

One particular grievance from a farmer—and not one of my father's favorite farmers, incidentally—regarded the destruction of his turnips by rabbits. Boasting of the size and quality of his crop, the farmer told my father, "The buggers are eetin the insides oot o' ma neeps an' sleepin in there." The terrain nearest the turnip patch consisted of a large sand bank riddled with rabbit holes and totally covered in whins (gorse), impenetrable even for a dog.

The plan devised was to burn the whins and clear the area to expose the rabbit holes. I accompanied Dad the following Saturday to the spot, and we set the hill ablaze. What a fearsome sight—flames leaping fifteen, twenty feet in the air. The inferno lasted close to an hour. We returned next day to a bleak, desolate area, only a few charred sticks protruding from the blackened ground. As Dad expected, there were too many holes even for bolt nets so, armed with two 12-bore, double-barreled shotguns (one borrowed from the neighboring gamekeeper) and his two trusty ferrets, he took up a stance on a rise overlooking the area. With both guns loaded and the rest of the shells so laid out that I could easily grab them in pairs, Dad gave the order. "Pit in the ferrets an' get ready, Loon." I ran back by my father, who was ready with one gun in hand while I held the other at arm's length.

A noticeable rumbling under our feet warned us that the ferrets had made contact with the rabbits. "Here they come, Loon." *Bang! Bang!* He grabbed the second gun from me, thrusting the spent one in my direction, never taking his eyes off the field. I cracked the breech, slammed in two fresh shells, and snapped it shut only seconds before it was yanked from my grasp. *Bang, Bang*, snap, reload, yank, *Bang, Bang … Bang, Bang … Bang, Bang.* My ears were ringing, my left hand burning from the heat of the barrels, but I dared not lift my eyes from the rhythmic task lest I lose my concentration.

The pace slowed gradually until the noise was overcome by a thankful silence and the acrid smell of gunpowder.

I retrieved the ferrets while Dad collected, gutted and paired the rabbits. They were loaded on our bicycles in pairs, slung over the handlebars and crossbars, twelve pair per bicycle, forty-eight rabbits in all.

As we trudged our way home, pushing our loads, a woman stuck her head out the door shouting, "Hiv yi ony spare rabbits, the day keeper?"

Dad never lifted his head. He just growled the reply. "No wifie. I hivna shot the spare anes yet."

THE RADIO

W e got our first radio, a small portable one, in 1939. My father received it as a Christmas gift from the Laird. The gamekeepers all received nice expensive gifts from him then—his way of showing appreciation for their work and loyalty.

The radio required two batteries; we referred to them as the wet battery and the dry battery. The wet battery (I think the proper name for it was the accumulator) was the same as today's car battery. The dry battery, some ten inches square and three inches thick, consisted of about a hundred small batteries all connected together to produce 120 volts. They were very expensive and didn't last long. The wireless, as it was called back then, had two stations—the home and the light.

Listening time was strictly regulated. The news, morning and night, was heard in silence. Only after it was finished could we talk about it.

Dad's program in the evening was the half-hour of Scottish dance music—Jimmy Shand, Bobby McLeoud, Angus Fitchet or Ian Powrie. In those days there was no way of knowing which band would be playing on a particular night, so there was always an air of anticipation as the time approached. On the evenings when The Strings of The B.B.C. was announced, Dad would explode into a volley of words descriptive of his dislike for the band and *click*, off went the wireless.

My mother's appointed time, at three in the afternoon, was the soap opera *Mrs. Dale's Diary*. She would make herself a cup of tea, get her writing pad, her fountain pen, and a handful of letters she needed to answer, switch on the wireless and start writing. She would still be writing long after the *click* that indicated the end of the program.

Yes, I was also granted time with the wireless—7:00 p.m., *Dick Barton, Special Agent*. As I write, I can still hear that signature theme song in the back of my head. Dick, Jock and Snowey solving crimes. The sound effects, the plot, the intrigue, painted a picture in my mind far superior to anything our modern-day, wide-screen, hi-def, digital, mumbo-jumbo TV set could ever come up with.

The wet batteries were the first to give out. Two were always needed—one in use and one on charge. Dad had crafted custom-made wooden boxes with leather carrying straps to transport them to and from the garage in the village where they were recharged for a fee or, more often than not, barter. As usual, it fell upon us youngsters to do the swap.

Cath and I were walking home one evening with the recharged battery. It was my turn to carry it. It was not very heavy, so I was swinging it back and forth in rhythm with my step when Cath suddenly shouted, "Dinna di that, ye'll mix up a the stations!"

This same battery system lasted for many, many years. Even when electricity became available to the majority of rural areas, the gamekeeper's cottage was usually still far beyond its reach. In fact, I never lived in a house with electricity until I got married at the age of twenty-four.

My older brother, Dodd, had acquired all kinds of knowledge while in the army, like Morse code, which he taught me in the evenings. Come my birthday, he presented me with a "buzzer," a keypad with a knob that enabled one to tap out Morse code messages. I got quite good at it, but could never come close to the speed at which he could receive and transmit.

A few years later I was introduced to the crystal set—a radio that didn't need batteries, but did need headphones. It belonged to a schoolmate of mine. He was not really a friend—a spoiled brat whose parents obviously had more money than sense, He had every toy and gadget money could buy, but not a shred of sense.

I really can't remember how this old edition of *Popular Mechanics* came into my possession, but it turned out to be quite a milestone in my life. I subscribed to it and had it shipped to me from America every month, and to this day I still receive it.

This magazine had the plans, drawings and easy-to-follow instructions to build your own crystal set. Except for the headphones, the plans called for materials I had on hand—cotton-covered bell wire, the cardboard tube from a toilet roll, a razor blade and some thumbtacks. I had it built long before I had the headphones to try it out. There were no shops, catalogs or army surplus stores back then that would carry the item.

One evening my brother Dodd came home from work and unceremoniously handed me a brown paper bag. "There ye go, Loon," was all he said.

There they were—a beautiful set of ex-Air Force headphones, used, but in good condition.

My crystal set worked better than I had ever dreamed. Plenty of volume. I could even change channels. My own radio! No longer was I restricted to my time slot on the house wireless or to the occasional outburst of "Turn that damned thing doon!" from Dad when listening to *Dick Barton*.

My father showed little or no interest in my projects, only the occasional, "Fit are ye trying at de noo?" as he glanced over my shoulder.

The evening of the big boxing match with Joe Louis and some contender finally arrived. It had been much talked about between Dad and my older brothers as to who was the better of the two fighters. I can still see dad taking off his boots and putting on his slippers, filling his pipe, settling back in his chair and turning on the wireless.

A few words from the announcer, Raymond Glendenning, then *crackle, crackle*. The battery went dead. Dad exploded with a hail of verbal abuse and accusation. Where was the extra battery? Well, why had it not been charged? He was devastated. A lull in the diatribe gave me the chance to offer him the use of my crystal set, but it didn't help much. "Fit good wid that damned thing be," he moaned.

"Foo nae gie it a try anyway, Dodd," my mother coaxed.

He was still moaning and groaning as I sat him on the edge of the bed in my room and slipped the headphones over his ears. The result was like a shot of morphine. I saw his body relax, his eyes close and his head slump forward a little. He has there at ringside. His right hand was giving little jabs accompanied by "*Oof ... Oof.*" I backed out of my bedroom leaving him to finish his fight.

He appeared some time later, smiling, and proceeded to give a blow-by-blow account of the whole match. When it was all over I felt it now safe to get Dad's opinion of my crystal set.

"Nae bad," was his only reply.

After he had settled back in his chair and lit his pipe, he turned round and looked at me.

"Nae batteries," I said. "Nae batteries."

MILITARY TACTICS

During our stay at Loch-Na-Bo in the early 1940s, it was difficult not to become involved in the daily routine of the army camp. My father was often befriended by the officers who lived in nearby quarters. He would invite them to come and listen to the news on the wireless in the evening (radios were banned in the camp). In return they would bring with them maybe a bag of flour or raisins, sometimes butter or the ultimate gift, tea.

As far as food was concerned the rationing did not affect us as much as it did the city dwellers. My father always planted a large vegetable garden. Wild ducks, geese and rabbits were always at hand, we had honey from his bees, and there were always a few trout from the loch. There were two rowboats available for hire to anyone who cared to pay the small fee to fish by the hour; no fishing from shore was allowed, and the ban was strictly enforced by my father. My mother was the booking agent and collector of fees.

Fly fishing only was the rule, with wet flies being the most popular. I never heard of anyone having much luck with dry flies. In the evenings I would sit and watch Dad tying all the varieties of his choice—March brown, teal and green, teal and gold, woodcock and gold, blae (blue) and black, the Zulu. But his all-time favorite was the butcher.

I would sometimes be asked to row the boat for anglers, and would be rewarded with a sixpence or even a shilling—an absolute fortune for me at that time—if I showed them the secret spots where the fish hung out. It was also my job to keep the boats free of water, so every morning before going to school I would have to remove the duck boards (floorboards) and bail the water out with a can.

At one time there was a regiment of Indians, or maybe they were Pakistanis, passing through the camp. They were mule handlers by profession. That was the first time I had ever seen a dark-skinned person. They were all very pleasant, always smiling, and they liked me a lot. They never stopped complaining about how cold it was, however. (This was midsummer, and the temperatures were close to 70 degrees.)

This particular morning when I went to bail out the boats, a small group of them, including two mules and an English officer, had assembled on the small concrete quay. It was their intention to experiment with an idea to get the mules and handlers to the other side of the loch. They had acquired the tubular steel framework and canvas cover from one of the big trucks. I watched with curiosity as they spread the canvas out on the concrete and then placed the inverted steel frame on top of it. "What are they up to now?" I wondered.

As they started to pull the tarp up the sides of the framework, it dawned on me. They were trying to build some kind of boat. Even at my tender age I could see the tarp was far too small, however.

The officer sped off in his jeep, returning with another tarp, and so the whole process was repeated using the two tarps end to end and folded over three or four times to form what was expected to be a waterproof seal.

The cover now securely lashed to the framework, the "boat" was slid into the water to test for leaks. I could not see the results from my vantage point but, judging by the cries of joy and the amount of backslapping, it must have been all right. To my surprise the officer slowly walked up to where I was seated and inquired in his beautiful, cultured, English accent if I was indeed the gamekeeper's son and, if so, could I inform my father that his presence was requested on the quay.

"Fit the hell wid he be wintin me for?" Dad asked no one as he slid into his jacket. Then he took off ahead of me as if I wasn't even there.

He reached the quay well ahead of me and was greeted with a hearty handshake and a "Good of you to come, old chap." From here on the conversation became muffled with only the occasional raised remark from Dad that sounded like "Ye stupid bugger!" or, now and then, "Di ye think I'm daft?" However, after a lot of waving of hands, pointing and gesturing, it all culminated in the officer placing his hand on Dad's shoulder, guiding him slowly out of earshot and talking to him in low inaudible tones. Whatever was said must have worked, because when he turned around my father was smiling.

He looked up to where I stood and shouted, "Go hame an get ma wee exie, Loon!" (The "wee exie" was his small hand axe.) When I returned with the axe, the mules and four of their trainers were already loaded into the makeshift boat. The officer was busy attaching a rope from the boat to the rowboat, where Dad was already seated at the oars. I handed him the axe, which he quickly slipped under the seat when he thought all eyes were diverted from him.

Off set the armada for the opposite shore. They had not gone very far when the mules made it quite clear they wanted no part in this maritime experience. It took every ounce of strength and training from their handlers to subdue them. Even then the contraption had definite list to starboard, and the wind had picked up.

My father, now minus his jacket, was straining at the oars, and even at this range I could detect some apprehension in his actions. I set off on foot at top speed around the loch to the opposite shore.

I arrived there just as the flotilla beached itself. The mules were released and took off into the woods somewhere. Their handlers didn't seem to care. They were on their knees apparently thanking somebody for something. The officer, his face green in some places, white in others, was trying to light a wet cigarette with hands shaking out of control.

I walked up to Dad. "Fit like?" I asked.

"Ach, nae bad, Loon."

He strolled over to the officer, who by now had regained most of his composure, and asked, "Are ye ready for me tae tak ye back ower, Captain?" The look of surprise (or was it fear?) on the captain's face was answer enough, but the officer, declining the offer, thanked him profusely, shook his hand over and over again and assured my father that his men would return the boat in the morning.

As Dad and I walked home I was itching to know, why the axe?

"Weel," he answered, "if that thing wis gan tae the bottom it wisna takin me wi it."

The axe was to sever the rope if need be.

That evening after dinner Dad answered a knock at the door. It was the captain. "Are you ready, Mister Stewart?" he enquired.

"All be richt wi ye, Captain," says Dad.

As he was closing the door, he stuck his head back in to tell Mam that he "wis jist gan ower tae the officers mess for wee whilie."

So that was what all the whispers and negotiations were about on the quay this morning.

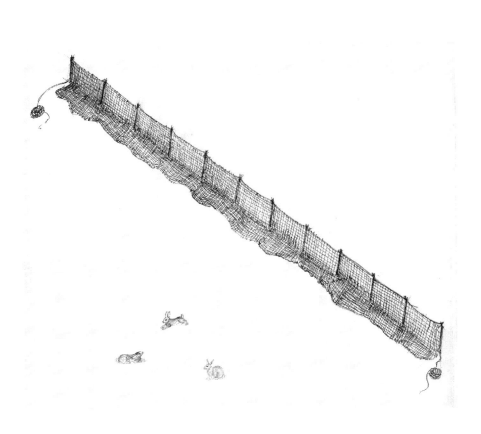

THE TACKLE NET

The rabbit population in Morayshire, Scotland, had reached plague proportions in the mid-1940s. They were breeding like, well, rabbits. All efforts to cull the numbers proved futile. Traps, snares, bolt nets, gassing and shooting were the methods of choice, but there was another method known to few, and used mostly by poachers (individuals who took game or fish illegally). It consisted of a huge net some fifty yards long and about three feet wide. The prime location to put this net to its fullest use would be a field next to a wooded area from which the rabbits would come out in hordes at dusk to feed.

To set the net, one would lay the net out on the ground stretched out to its full length as closely as possible to the woods, and leave it there for a few days to allow the rabbits to get used to it. It was almost invisible lying there in the grass.

A couple of dozen small posts—maybe thirty inches long and a half to three-quarters of an inch round—and two large balls of string completed the tackle. The posts were sharpened to a point on one end, while the other had a notch cut in it. They would be pushed into the ground beside the net and spaced about six feet apart throughout the length of the net. The first and last stakes had a ball of twine attached to them and left there in readiness for the big night.

The operation required two people and was carried out in complete darkness. Thus, it was of great importance that each person had a good mental picture of the field in daylight.

The rabbits out in the field feeding were not easily frightened at night. If they suspected an approaching danger, they would just cower down, their ears flat against their backs, and stay there until it passed.

On the night of the operation, one man would start at the beginning of the net, picking it up by one edge and hanging it on the notch in the top of the post, then on to the next one and so on until the whole net was hung up on the posts. The net being quite a bit wider than the height of the posts allowed it to form a sort of bag on the ground. When your partner reached the far end of the net, he would give three tugs on it to alert you that he was ready to continue.

You would pick up the ball of string and start paying it out, but keeping it taut, as you walked slowly round the perimeter of the field, passing each other on the edge of the field opposite the net. You brushed the grass with the string with sweeping movements, paying out or hauling in string as needed, each one heading back to the opposite end of the net from which he started. When you got there, you kept hauling on the strings.

The rabbits seldom panicked. They would just keep hopping ahead of the advancing string, which was pushing them closer and closer to the net. Not until they found themselves on top of each other would they decide something was definitely wrong. Then panic sets in, a mad dash for the woods and safety. The net, now blocking their retreat, would become a seething, screeching, squealing, tangled mass of fur.

You would then drop the ball of string and throw yourselves at the squirming, scratching animals, untangling, snapping necks as fast as you could in the darkness. Most of the work is done only by feel. It would take a long time to empty the net and pick it up into a heap to be untangled in daylight. The rabbits would have to wait until then, too.

After one such night my father and I returned at daybreak the next morning, nursing our sores (rabbit scratches are very painful, and easily become infected, too, if you are not careful), and collected our tackle. It took some time to gut and pair the fifty-odd rabbits we got from the haul—a good night's work. Exciting, too, and put quite a dent in the rabbit population. I helped my father on a few of these hunts and really enjoyed them.

My close friend Bob Wildegoose and I were always up to some kind of scheme. We both had air rifles and, since his father owned their farm, legal rabbit hunting was never a problem. Any given day during school holidays would find us scouring the whin bushes for rabbits. When we got a few, we would flag down the butcher's van while he was on his door-to-door mission selling his products. He was always glad of a few extra rabbits, and I'm sure the money he gave us for them, although a handsome amount, was far below the wholesale price.

We thought we could really make a killing if we could up the number of rabbits we caught. "The tackle net," I suggested. "Yes!" And Bob already had the perfect location in mind—a remote field up by "The Crows Wood." I said I would take care of the net, boasting a little, and then regretting the statement a little, too, as I cycled home.

My father had three such nets hanging in the shed, confiscated from poachers. To think of asking to borrow one was totally out of the question, so I had to wait for the opportunity when no one was around to secretly remove it and stash it at Bob's farm.

We set out the net one evening. The field looked perfect. The grass had been nibbled down to bowling green quality, indicating a large rabbit population. We took time to get the layout of the field in our minds because, when we returned in a few nights, it would be in complete darkness.

When that night came, I went ahead and quietly set up the net, dreaming of the haul we were going to take. I gave the three tugs on the net and started sweeping.

We passed each other on the opposite side of the field without saying a word.

The first indication I had that something might be wrong was when my string hung up on something, then released itself. When it happened a second time I wondered, what could it be? We had just about completed the maneuver when I got my answer.

Baaaaaa ... Baaa ... Baaaa ...

Unknown to either Bob or me, his father had put about twenty sheep in the field that day. *Baaaa ... Baaaaaaaa ...* And now they were in our net.

What a mess. Squirming sheep, rabbits, tangled net, *Baaaaa ... Baaa ...,* total darkness. We tried to separate the sheep. Forget about the rabbits! *Baaaaaa ...* I got kicked in the mouth, twice. We had to give up and return next morning.

Luckily, the sheep were none the worse for their nocturnal experience, but the net did not fare so well. It was ripped to shreds (but we did get two rabbits).

I returned the net to its former place beside the other two, exactly where I had taken it from.

I thought this would be the end of the saga until one day I came home from school to find my father deep in negotiation with Geordie Grant, the tenant of the farm "Pittensair."

Now, it was quite legal for farmers to use the tackle net on their own farms; however, I am not so sure of the legality of bartering for a confiscated net. My father boasted of the pristine condition of the said net.

I had to look away and hum a tune to myself as Dad unfolded the net for Geordie's inspection. My father, horrified at the condition of the net and full of apologies, offered Geordie his choice of the other two nets.

I think the deal did go gown between them, but that night at the supper table Dad kept going on and on about the ripped-up net and asking no one in particular what had caused it.

I thought about suggesting rats had got into it, but that might lead to further cross-examination, on which I had no chance against my father, so I just kept my mouth shut and thanked my lucky stars I had got away with what I had.

THE POLE VAULT

At school during our play time, boys would have all different kinds of games or activities, which were usually divided into "seasons" that lasted from a few days to a week or two.

There was the kite season, for instance. Most of us would make some attempt at building one at home and take it to school to show it off and put it through its paces. They were generally rough-looking things, mostly made from newspaper and long slivers of wood split from any piece of board we could lay our hands on. Brown sticky paper two inches wide, which had to be moistened (usually by one's tongue), was the only material I could think of at that time to fasten the paper to the framework. The string to fly it with was usually binder twine used in a tractor-drawn machine to tie the sheaves of grain. Almost every farm had one of these machines, and since most of the boys were sons of farmers, there was always a good supply of the rough hairy stuff. I could get enough for my kite for only ten .303 bullet cases.

When the kite flying season had run its course, there was always the slingshot season (we called them "catapults"), the cricket season, rounders (similar to baseball), and the rubber-band gun season. These guns were also crafted at home and taken to school and shown off with pride, sometimes to the envy of one's less-gifted classmates.

The gun would consist of a pistol-shaped piece of wood with a flat back to the handgrip where a spring clothes peg was attached. A rubber band, usually cut from an old bicycle inner tube, was clamped in the clothes peg by one end and the other end was stretched over the muzzle. On squeezing the clothes peg, the band would be released to a distance of fifteen feet or more.

The bow and arrow season was always good for a couple of weeks or more. These were homemade, mostly from rose bushes if you could find one thick enough; if not, just about any kind of stick would do, with the usual binder twine for the string. The only wood we used for arrows were the canes from wild raspberry bushes, which grew everywhere. There was no need for fletching (adding feathers to the shaft); they worked fine without them. However, the empty brass case of a 9-millimeter bullet slipped on the point gave it a better balance, and looked impressive too. (I could swap a dozen arrows for half that number in bullet casings.)

We would pick sides and have pitched battles, cowboy and Indian style, the cowboys having the rubber-band guns. No one was ever seriously hurt in these skirmishes, but looking back it would have been so easy to lose an eye.

We even had a season for the pole vault, for which I humbly claim to have been the instigator. Never did we use the crossbar thing for height as in the real competitions. We were content to leap onto the roof of the shelter shed or soar over the six-foot-high stone wall that separated the boys' playground from the girls'. The burn, six or seven feet wide, that ran through the woods behind the school was the greatest challenge. Many a boy had to sit through the afternoon class with wet feet or worse.

This whole pole vault thing started with me one Saturday when my younger sister and I accompanied Mam and Dad to the Keith Show. This was an annual event, mostly for farmers who would show their prize animals, compete in horse-handling skills, tractor-handling skills and displays of the most up-to-date implements and machines. There was horse racing, too, and bicycle races.

The "heavy events"—tossing the caber, the sheaf, throwing the hammer and the 56-pound weight over the bar—were always big attractions. Individual farms would train for weeks for the tug-of-war and compete against each other on this day.

The pole vault caught my attention. I was hooked. Nothing else deserved my attention for the rest of the day. I watched in awe and wonder as, one after the other, competitors soared so gracefully over the bar. During a lull in the competition, I wandered over there and started firing questions at them. They appeared impressed by my interest in the sport and even let me handle one of the poles. I found out later that this was a relatively new sport for the Keith Show.

On the journey home as I sat in the back seat of the Austin Seven, my head was filled with visions of gliding over dykes and fences, escaping the wrath of my older sisters by leaping to a rooftop, and from now on crossing the burn would never be a problem. As soon as the car came to a standstill, I was out, into my room, changed my clothes and off like a shot to find the pole I needed.

The house we lived in at this time was situated in a bare, desolate location, hardly a tree in sight. Finding a vaulting pole was going to be a challenge.

Yes! My eyes fell on the "clais (clothes) stretcher," not to be confused with a "clais pole." A clais pole is the post, about eight feet tall, to which the clothes line is attached. Two are required. The clais stretcher is a long slender pole about ten to twelve feet long with a notch in the smaller end to fit over the clothes line, which usually sagged in the middle when the wash line was loaded with clais. The clais stretcher would then be notched onto the center of the line and hoisted up to take full advantage of the breeze, with the lower end resting on the ground.

What a find! Perfect. From then on the clais stretcher became a vaulting pole until my mother, after much searching more than once, complained to my father, who immediately banned the use of the clais stretcher for any purpose other than that for which it was intended.

Undaunted, I found myself another pole. I became quite proficient at leaping onto and over obstacles. I loved the rush of excitement I would get from a fast run, planting the pole and soaring up and up to almost a stall, then slowly gaining speed down to the ground again. That pole went with me everywhere until some other activity took its place in my life.

It wasn't until a few years later, when I had to do my two years of National Service in the British Army as part of the Royal Engineers stationed in a training camp near Stratford-on-Avon, England, that I had the opportunity to reacquaint myself with the pole vault.

It was required that everyone in the squad take part in the upcoming camp sports. I was not really into sports, but I put my name down for the pole vault anyway.

When sports day came I went down to the field as a spectator. I had never heard from anyone as to whether I was competing or not, so I just assumed they had forgotten about me. It was announced over the sound system that the following such-and-such competitors should report to the pole vault area. I wasn't paying much attention, but one of my buddies shouted over to me, "Good luck, Ron!" which brought me to my senses.

I ambled over there to find at least a dozen other competitors, all in proper sports gear, limbering up, some doing sit-ups, others checking out the poles or pacing off the distance from there to somewhere. There was an officer there with an official-looking clipboard and a whistle on a string around his neck viewing the situation.

A blast from his whistle brought us all running in his direction. He started to call out names, to which we would answer, "SAH!"

The roll call completed, he laid down the rules. Every man was allowed three tries. If anyone felt confident they could clear the bar at the present height, they could shout, "Pass!" in order to save time and speed things up. After every man had had his turn, the bar would be raised a predetermined height.

I just stood there like a dummy. "You are going to make a right fool of yourself today, Ron," I thought to myself.

"What height shall we start at, chaps?" says the man with the whistle. There was a brief discussion among the competitors (I was not included), and someone shouted out, "Five feet, Sah!"

Was I hearing right? I think I could jump higher than that without a pole.

The competition began. To my pleasant surprise some of them were knocking the bar over and were eliminated even at that height. When my name was called I shouted, "Pass!"

Until now no one realized I was even in the competition. The whistle man queried, "Pass?"

"Pass," I answered, which brought a few snickers and giggles from competitors and spectators alike.

Five feet six—pass. Five feet nine—pass. Six feet—pass.

At that point there were only three competitors left in the running. One of them, who appeared to be quite good, shouted out, "Six feet six!" He was the only one who cleared it.

The officer walked over to where I stood in full uniform including my beret. He wore a sneering smile. "No pass this time, my good man. You must vault."

I didn't even take off my jacket, made a short run, up and over and landed on my feet.

A loud cheer went up from the crowd. My only remaining competitor rushed over and shook my hand vigorously, but I could tell from the look in his eyes it was all showmanship. "It's your call, mate," he announced.

Okay. If you want showmanship, I will give you showmanship, I thought.

I picked up the pole and walked to the point where I would start my run, looking back over my shoulder from time to time as I slowed my pace to a stop. I stood there for a minute or two, basking in the silence that had fallen on the field.

"Eight feet!" I shouted.

There was a gasp from the crowd as I stood there, my pole poised, waiting until they changed the height of the bar. As I started my run, gaining speed, I was fully confident I could do it easily. My balance was perfect, up and over, clearing the bar by at least two feet. I didn't even lose my beret when I landed.

This time the crowd went wild, almost a standing ovation.

I dusted myself off as I picked myself up. It was not really necessary, but that is what everyone else did, and I thought it might add a little flair to my performance. The officer with the clipboard and whistle announced my competitor's name and beckoned him onto the field. He walked halfway onto the field, viewed the bar, shook his head and walked off.

The officer bounced over to me, grabbed my hand, dragged me into full view, shot my right hand in the air and shouted, "The winner!" This time his facial expression was totally different. He had brought himself down to my level. "Good to have you in the regiment, old chap," he said with genuine affection. I was surrounded by a bunch of total strangers all eager to thank me and commend me on my performance. (The last competitor was not one of them.) The whistle officer suggested (commanded?) I stay close by for the awards ceremony at the end of the day.

A large crowd had gathered for the occasion as winner after winner was recognized. I was still a little in shock over the whole thing. What was the big deal? I only did what I had enjoyed doing when I was a lad.

"And now!" shouted the announcer, "the winner of the pole vault, with the impressive height of eight feet, Sapper Stewart!"

Once more the crowd burst into a volley of cheers and handclapping as I mounted the stage to accept my trophy (a ten-shilling voucher I could cash in at the N.A.F.F.I.). It was presented to me by an elderly gentleman in civilian clothes, whom I thanked as I shook his hand. As I made my way off stage, I was met by my regimental sergeant major who barked out, "See me first thing in my office tomorrow!"

Visions of a promotion, perhaps?

I presented myself to the clerk in the morning, all polished and shiny.

"Wait here," he said with no expression as he knocked on the door and entered the office.

"The major will see you now," he said, and in a quieter tone, "Take off your beret."

I came to attention in front of the sergeant's desk and waited … and waited … and waited … while he finished writing whatever it was.

Suddenly he took off his glasses, pushed his chair back violently and exploded into a volley of abuse directed at me. Well, the number of adjectives he used to describe me, accompanied by the amount of things he was going to have done to me, would fill another page. Something to do with not saluting my commanding officer while I was in uniform. How was I supposed to know that that old fuddy-duddy in civvies was my C.O.?

All this for ten bob.

D-DAY

Our stay at Loch-Na-Bo was very pleasant and memorable. Living in the middle of the army camp had its advantages. We made new friends every few weeks, and old friends that were there most of the time became almost like family.

Their living quarters consisted mainly of Nissen (Quonset) huts, dozens of them, scattered throughout the surrounding woods. My father was told that in the camp's infancy it was all tents, with no huts at all.

During the warm summer months, when the water in the loch receded quite a bit, my favorite pastime was searching the shores by wading out as far as I could to find all kinds of treasures—boxes of ammunition, a bayonet, cap badges, dishes, cups, saucers, etc.—all wonderful stuff to barter at school. One day I found a stash of beer bottles, all full. I took a couple home with me to show Dad, who sampled one right there and then. He was not really a drinking man, but did enjoy a dram or a beer as long as someone else was paying for it. I knew from the licking of lips and the smile that it met with his approval. "Is there ony mair doon there?" he queried.

I somehow neglected to tell him of the supply I had found, half-buried in the mud. I had moved as much as I could to a place where I could get at it easily when the loch's water table returned to normal. If I needed a favor of him or needed to borrow a tool, I somehow always managed to "find" a bottle for him then.

On overhearing a conversation between my father and one of the older officers who had seen the birth of the camp, it appears that the N.A.A.F.I. (the commissary), which was just a big tent at that time, had been blown down in a terrible windstorm and much of the merchandise was never recovered in the aftermath, thus my supply of beer.

As the years slipped by the camp grew proportionately. There were more and more soldiers, but it became less and less personal. You had just gotten to know someone when they would be replaced by some complete stranger.

There was a noted increase in the amount of gunfire, explosions, the rattle of tanks, sirens and shouting, even throughout the night. Perhaps you can imagine living in this environment and then waking up one morning to a dead silence. The hubbub of camp life never affected my sleep, but the awful silence of this morning had me bolt upright in bed before daylight.

I could hear low murmurings from Mam and Dad, who were already up, so I joined them in the living room to ask, "Fits' goin on?" No answer. Dad went outside in silence. No one spoke. My sisters had joined us by then. Dad returned after a few minutes, visibly upset. "Maybe Jerry has landed," he said, not a smile on his face. I felt a rush of adrenaline race through me as I envisioned pictures of prison camps with jackbooted guards holding rifles.

"I'm goin tae tack a look," he said. Grabbing the shotgun and stuffing shells into his jacket pocket, he disappeared out the door.

He was gone all of half an hour. He unloaded the gun and put it back in the rack before he addressed the sea of anxious faces. He was wearing the same expression as when he had left.

While he was gone my mother had busied herself preparing breakfast, the usual oatmeal and toast. During the meal Dad told of his walk round the camp. It was completely deserted, not a soul. Most of the stores and equipment was gone except for one or two trucks that seemed to be in need of repair. We had no clue as to what had happened.

"I'll tack the kids up tae the school," he said, as he donned his jacket and grabbed the gun.

He left us at the school gate and headed for home. We trooped into the classroom and took our seats. The headmaster, Charley Keith, strolled in. No "Good morning," he just walked up to the blackboard, chalk in hand, stared at it for a few seconds, then started scrawling two lines on it, a few inches apart, wider at the ends. Has the world gone mad, I wondered? He replaced the chalk by the board, turned around and faced us. Why all the dramatics?

He inquired if anyone had any idea what the two lines represented. Not a clue.

"Does anyone know what is going on in the war?" he asked.

"There's a lot o' fightin'," someone answered. Charley was unimpressed, but went on to explain that his two lines represented the south coast of England and the north coast of France. He explained that the Jerrys had already conquered most of Europe, and that we could be next in line.

Dad might have been right this morning, I thought.

He went on to tell us that the strip of water called the English Channel was the only obstacle the Jerrys had to overcome in order to invade us. I broke out in a cold sweat, but he went on to tell us that that very morning a massive British invasion was in progress to halt the German invasion and to drive them back. It was to be known as D-Day.

I think we all had to stifle a "Whoopee!"

So that's where everyone went this morning.

THE BICYCLE

B ack in the early 1940s during the war, getting around was not easy. The few choices you had were walking, taking the bus or train, private car, or bicycle. Most people who lived in the country walked from place to place. The nearest village was about four miles from where we lived. This was not a long walk compared to what some other people faced.

Saturday afternoon would find my mother and father off to Elgin, the bigger town some eight miles distant, to do the shopping for the week. They would have to walk about a mile to where they could get a bus to town. Quite often the bus would be full and would not stop, leaving them an hour to wait for the next one.

There were very few private cars around then. The doctor had one. Two or three of the big shop owners from town or the owners of the bigger farms also had cars, and that was about all there were in the area.

The bicycle, therefore, was the main mode of travel, the prized possession of anyone who owned one. It served as a means of getting to and from work or play. Keeping it in good working condition was always a priority. In the event of a breakdown, you were dead in the water. Without your bicycle you had no means of getting to work in the morning.

There was no electricity at this time, no shed or workshop in which to repair it. So, after dinner the table was moved back, some sheets of paper were laid on the floor, and the bike was brought into the living room where it was placed upside-down on the floor in order to be worked on. Usually it was a flat (or puncture, we called it) or a loose chain.

Major repairs were left until the weekend, if possible, when one could work on it in daylight. When parts were needed, a trip to the town dump was always fruitful. Brake blocks, chains, tires and tubes, pedals, sprockets, etc., found their way into my burlap sack and were stored for future use.

With as many as five or six bicycles in the family at any given time, there were few nights without a bicycle in the middle of the floor.

There were a couple of repair shops—one in the village (Lhanbryde), the other in Elgin—where the less capable could take them to be repaired. This involved days, weeks, of waiting. All the capable men were at war, and parts were difficult to get. Shipping took forever. The repair shop in the village was also the shoemaker. He had a wooden leg and was known as "Kempie."

Not everyone had a bicycle. Even a used one was very expensive, if you could find one. We all had bicycles in our family, however, thanks to my father.

At this time we lived at Loch-Na-Bo in the middle of an army camp, so when my father was making his rounds during the day he quite often found a bicycle abandoned by some soldier who had stolen it in order to get back to camp before curfew. In addition to being a gamekeeper, my father was also in the special police, a voluntary organization to supplement the regular force that was short of manpower.

On finding a bicycle he would have to take it to the police station in Elgin, where it would be kept until it was claimed. A few would be claimed, but there was never any real attempt to advertise a found bicycle. Anyone going there to claim their bicycle would be asked to show the number (all bikes were numbered then) and give a full description before they saw it. Only then would they get it back.

If no one claimed it after eight weeks, my father got it. In order to get the bicycle to Elgin, and there being no transport available, he became quite proficient at riding his own bike with his left hand while guiding the other one alongside with his right. After he had fitted out the family with bicycles, he would take any new ones he found to the mart where he sold them.

All bicycles were required to have a front and rear light. This law was strongly enforced by the police and could result in a hefty fine if you were caught without lights on your bike. I recall one night cycling home accompanied by my younger sister from an evening's dancing when the local Bobbie pulled alongside of us and asked my sister where her rear light was. We thought he was joking, but no. He told us to pull over and asked us where we had been and where we were going. He wrote down my sister's name then asked me for mine. "What for?" I asked. "A witness," says he. He compared the two names. "You her brother?" he asked. I told him I was, to which he added, "I thought you were her boyfriend." The incident cost her ten shillings.

The lights on your bike were always a problem. The battery-operated ones never lasted very long, and you would sometimes forget to switch them off. The ones that were powered by a little generator (we called it "a dynamo") were more dependable. This generator was mounted on a spring bracket attached to the bicycle frame in such a way that the small pulley would ride on the tire. This worked quite well except on rainy nights when, at a certain speed, the pulley would lose traction on the wet wheel and the light would go out. I thought I had the perfect answer when I slipped the thick rubber washer from a screw-top beer bottle over the small pulley. It worked as well as I expected until, coming home one night in the pouring rain at full speed, everything suddenly went black. I braked as hard as I could, too late to stop me from getting entangled in a barbed-wire fence. Getting out of there was no small task. I had numerous painful scratches, and getting my bike out took even longer. When I got home my mother nearly died. I was totally covered in blood, and the rain made it look a lot worse than it really was.

The number of hours one would spend straddling that bicycle was unbelievable. It was more than an hour going to work, and the same coming home. Besides, I might be sent to a job ten miles beyond the workshop, leaving me with a twenty-mile ride home at the end of the day.

Mileage was seldom a problem, however. In fact, it was quite a pleasure most of the time. Rain was a nuisance, but didn't bother me very much since I had the proper raingear. The wind was my worst enemy. A strong headwind could double travel time, and fatigue always accompanied it.

I had a strong, heavy bicycle made by Elswick. It had a four-speed transmission in the hub of the rear wheel, and the gear change was activated by a fine steel cable connected to a trigger on the handlebars. A generator was built into the hub of the front wheel—no more problems in wet weather. A strong rack with a spring clamp like a mousetrap was mounted over the rear wheel and served to carry raingear, tools, etc. A mall leather pouch containing a few spanners and a puncture repair outfit hung under the saddle. The transmission, in my mind, was an engineering marvel. The tiny planetary gears and pawls always fascinated me, so it did not take me long to find the secrets of the workings. I could strip, repair and rebuild a Sturmy Archer transmission in an evening.

The lighter racing bicycles had a different kind of transmission, a series of different-sized sprockets with a means to move the chain over from one to the other. Not too many tradesmen favored this type of bicycle. It was too light and fragile for the loads they were expected to carry, and few people could afford a second bicycle for sports use only.

Most accidents on bicycles were either self-inflicted or from contact with a motorized vehicle. (I have never heard of a head-on crash between two bicycles.)

Speaking of self-inflicted: Most nights, returning home from work I would take a shortcut around the village of Garmouth that involved negotiating a winding foot path about two feet wide. I would approach it at full speed and pretend I was on a race track, ahead of the pack, in full control. As I rounded a curve, almost horizontal with the road, I was confronted by a baker's van in my path. No time to think, a sudden swerve to the left brought me in contact with a stone wall. *Wham*! I ended up on the opposite side of the wall, a bit shaken up, but no serious injuries.

I examined my bike and found that the impact had been so great that the frame was bent to the extent that the front wheel would not clear it when I turned the handlebars. To add insult to injury, the driver of the baker's van, who had a customer at the time, exclaimed, "Straighten it oot, Loon, affore it gets cauld." Although his remark didn't amuse me, I did take his advice since it was the only obvious thing to do under the circumstances. I pushed on the back of the front wheel with my foot while pulling back on the handlebars with both hands until I had enough clearance to make the bike ride-able.

My father, the wheeler-dealer that he was, talked "Kempie" into replacing my damaged frame with a used one he had in stock, so within a week I was mobile again.

However, this was not the end of the saga. A few months later I was coming home from work on a Friday night laden with tools needed for a job on the weekend. Halfway home, everything went black. Then, I regained consciousness for a few minutes. I was lying on the road with a few men around me asking questions. I blacked out again. When consciousness returned I was in an ambulance, I blacked out again almost immediately.

When I recovered, I was in a hospital bed with my mother and father at my bedside. I can't remember any of the conversation that evening. It was not until the following morning that my memory started to return. I can remember a Bobby asking me many times if I had been struck by another vehicle, to which my answer was a definite "no."

When they examined my bicycle at the police station, they discovered that the front wheel and forks had broken off completely from the rest of the column. They said it had been cracked for quite some time and finally gave out, sending me face-first into the roadway.

I spent two weeks in the hospital recovering from a severe concussion, but I fully recovered and was back to work in no time. Apparently, when my bicycle was rebuilt after the first crash, the crack had gone unnoticed.

This same bicycle served me well for many years. Before I left Scotland I gave my bike to my father to use or dispose of as he wished.

One evening I sat down with a pencil to calculate the distance I had covered on my bicycles and came up a staggering figure of over 150,000 miles.

THE WOODS

I left school at thirteen years old when school ended for the year and the summer holidays began. I had the whole summer ahead of me to fish, hunt, or do any other sport or project that came to mind.

My hopes were dashed at the supper table that evening when my father announced that he had spoken to Harry Morrison that day and had gotten me a full-time job working in the woods as one of his crew. I would start off stacking brush and could advance on to be a woodsman (lumberjack). I would be starting on Monday.

This was the last kind of job I had in mind for my future, but to complain would have been useless, to say the least. I thanked Dad without showing too much enthusiasm and agreed to the job.

It was only half a mile to the pine plantation where Harry and his five men were engaged in a thinning operation. Every other tree or so was felled by two of the crew with a long saw that had a handle at each end. The other men followed with axes and cut off all the branches at what I considered lightning speed. These trees averaged twenty-five feet in height and three to six inches in diameter. It was my job to drag the branches and stack them in rows about twenty feet apart, where they were left to rot or provide a habitat for wildlife.

As the weeks flew by I became quite proficient with the axe or on the saw. I was known as "the Loon" (the kid), but was expected to keep up with the men.

We moved from wood to wood wherever the next contract landed us. We were not always working on plantations; sometimes we would take down huge trees—hard and dangerous work. When working on the bigger trees, it was customary for men to cut a cross in the stump with only four strokes of the axe, each one precisely aimed at an angle so that the chip would come out clean. Every time it rained the cut would fill up with water, which would speed the decay of the stump. The cuts were a signature of the woodsman, because there were never two crosses alike cut by different woodsmen.

I had been secretly practicing the cuts and was quite confident I could match any of the others. My opportunity came one day when the subject came up as we sat round the campfire having our sandwiches and tea. Each man claimed that he was better than the other, so it was decided there and then that there would be a competition to decide who was best. It appeared that I was not going to be asked to take part, so I told them I would like to compete also.

I was amazed at the response. They shook my hand, patted my back and unanimously agreed that I should be allowed to go first. They ushered me over to the nearest tree stump while one of them busied himself clearing the area of branches and other debris. I was even given a choice of axes. (Normally no one would dare touch the axe of a fellow worker.)

I cut a perfect cross, to the delight of the men. There was more handshaking and back-patting, then one of them summoned the boss, Harry Morrison, to come and take a look. He ambled over and gazed at my handiwork. "Nae bad. But could ye do it blindfolded?" he asked, not a smile on his face.

The crew gathered round me again with lots of encouraging words to the effect that I could do it "Nae bother." Someone produced a handkerchief as they guided me in the direction of a fresh stump. I was overwhelmed by all this newfound affection, but was enjoying every minute of it.

"Tak aff yer jacket," somebody suggested, and two eager helpers removed it just as the blindfold was tightened over my eyes. Many hands gently lined me up with the stump, assuring me that I had perfect alignment.

"Wait a minute," says Harry, as he took me by the shoulders and realigned me another few degrees. "Go for it, Loon," says he.

Dead silence. Then *whack … whack*!

A loud cheer went up. There was more backslapping and words of praise as they gently rotated me the necessary forty-five degrees to complete the cross.

Whack … Whack!

Another, louder cheer broke the silence. Yes!! "Well done," I heard, as I felt fingers undo the blindfold. This had to be one of the most memorable days of my life. Accepted into manhood, now I would be one of them. No more "Loon."

The blindfold was off, but why had everyone retreated, and why the dead silence?

I looked down at the stump expecting to see a perfect cross. Horror of horrors!

There lay the sleeve of my jacket, sliced to shreds. The buggers!

After I had been blindfolded, they had laid the sleeve of my jacket over the stump. The whole thing had been planned ahead of time, of course. These things are common practice in any trade. I suppose it is meant to make you stronger, to make you humble, to make you not so sure of yourself—in my opinion, a tradition that should never be allowed to die.

I spent at least two years in the woods. I enjoyed the open air, and most of the time you had no one looking over your shoulder. I experienced almost every aspect of the logging industry, even to the art of skidding out the timbers with horses (another story, perhaps) and to running a "prop mill" (where the smaller trees were cut into pit props for the coal mines)—all nothing more than hard, backbreaking work.

Then one night we were once again sitting around the campfire at dinnertime. Harry wasn't there; he had chronic asthma, which required him to miss quite a few days of work. In his absence we had the opportunity to discuss the present wage table which, it was unanimously agreed, was way below what we should be receiving.

Scott, one of the crew whom I had grown to respect for his wisdom and consideration for others, addressed me with the question of why a bright, educated young man like myself should be following such a dead-end job like this. "You should be following a trade, serving an apprenticeship, instead of wasting your time around here."

I agreed with him wholeheartedly, but explained that I had been following every lead available, to no avail.

"Nonsense," says he, "Smith and Gordon, up at The Crofts of Dipple was lookin' for a loon tae serve an apprenticeship wi' them as a jiner [carpenter]. It was in the paper on Setterday."

Well, we never get a paper on Saturday, but I took him at his word and, after getting the directions to The Crofts of Dipple, I mounted my bike and was off right there and then to see if I could secure the job.

I reached this ramshackle, rundown building, which resembled a chicken house more than a carpenters' shop, but the sign, faded from years of exposure, assured me that this, indeed, was Smith and Gordon, carpenter and joiners.

The door was already open, so I entered rather timidly to see two dungaree-clad individuals deeply engrossed over some very large sheets of paper on a workbench already laden with tools and some half-assembled work pieces. They turned round, a little surprised at my entrance and, before they could comment, I exclaimed, "Are ye lookin' for a loon tae be a jiner?"

Well, the long and the short of it was, only after a myriad of questions on my education, family, where I lived and what my father worked at did I fully realize the five-year commitment I was about to enter. Geordie turned to Alex and said, "I think we should gie 'im the job."

It was agreed that I should start the following Monday. They both seemed very happy with their selection, and even at that point I felt that I was genuinely accepted. I sped back to my woodsmen colleagues who were sitting exactly where I had left them over two hours before. I broke the news to them as to what had happened. In low tones they congratulated me and were completely in support of my decision, especially Scott, who claimed responsibility for my good fortune.

That evening at the supper table I broke the news to the family. Everyone was glad for me and congratulated me for the way I had taken the bull by the horns and pursued the job of my dreams. Only my father was a little reserved. Although not disappointed, he thought that my choice of future employment should rest in law enforcement.

"Ye should go for the bobbies, Loon," was his input.

FEAR

There are two kinds of fear—fear of what you know, and fear of what you don't know. Here are a couple of examples.

At this time we were living at a place called "The Bungalow Corbiewells" a couple of miles from Garmouth, an open, windswept location. Farms all around us, and hardly a tree in sight.

The winds of March would bring sandstorms—sand in our beds, sand in the cupboards, even sand in our food.

Most of the farms kept sheep so, come lambing season, wild dogs were always a big problem. They were not really wild dogs, just domestic dogs that had been abandoned and gone wild. They would pack up in twos or threes to attack a herd of sheep and would kill just for the joy of killing, sometimes wounding more than they killed. But the real damage was caused when pregnant ewes lost their lambs from the trauma of the attack.

It was my father's job to take care of the problem. So random were these raids, and communications being what they were—usually someone sent on a bicycle to summon the gamekeeper—by the time he got there the dogs were always gone.

My older brother, George (Dodd), worked as a security officer at the naval air base about seven miles from us and did the commute on his 350 A.J.S. motorcycle. One evening coming home from work, he screeched into our driveway in a cloud of dust shouting, "Dad, there's twa dogs in the sheep up by the crossroads!" "A'll get the gun," says Dad, retreating into the house. They took off in another cloud of dust with Dad straddling the pillion.

They were back within half an hour, driving much slower this time with Dodd holding the shotgun across the handlebars. My father had a dead dog slung across his shoulders and was holding onto the bike with his knees. They dumped the dog at the back door and Dad covered it up with a burlap sack, and there it stayed.

As usual, I had to wait until suppertime to get the story. Dad and my brother took turns telling the tale, painting a graphic portrait of the whole episode.

It appears that, when they reached the crossroads, Dodd skidded to a stop, threw the latch off the gate, pushed it open with the front wheel, opened the throttle, and took off. "Efter them, Loon," shouted my father as they charged over the rugged terrain, slowly closing in on the dogs.

"Haud her steady there, Loon," said he in a remarkably calm voice considering the situation. *Blam*! The black dog rolls over in a lifeless heap. *Blam*! The second dog heads for the woods dragging a leg.

After we had eaten and the table was cleared, only then was everyone allowed to troop out to see the dog. My father pulled off the burlap sack to reveal a muscular, pointy-eared animal with slits where its eyes should be. This was not like any dog I had ever seen.

Dad reached forward and with both hands opened the dog's mouth.

I froze. My knees buckled, the hair on the back of my neck stood on end. I looked at the teeth. These were not teeth; they were fangs.

That vision will remain in my mind for as long as I live.

It was a few years after this that we moved to a place called "Loch of Cotts," an old stone cottage with a slate roof, surrounded on three sides by a pine forest. It overlooked a large area of marshland which, at one time, might have been the loch. A dirt driveway about a mile long through the forest connected us to the main road.

I was serving a five-year apprenticeship as a carpenter at this time and had to cycle the eight miles or so to and from work every day, including Saturdays when we worked a half-day. My Saturday routine never changed much. When I came home from work, had my dinner (dinner was always midday; supper was the evening meal), changed from my dungarees to my flannels, got back on my bicycle and was off to Elgin.

I had a half-hour fiddle lesson at two o'clock, then off to the "Picture House" to see a movie after I had put my fiddle in the left luggage at the bus station. Fish and chips next, and off to the "Playhouse" to watch another movie before cycling home.

If it was bad weather, I would ride with Mam and Dad in the Austin Seven when they went to do their weekly shopping, and then take the bus home. The bus route terminated at the end of our road, so I had to walk the last mile through the trees to the house.

It was on one of these late, dark nights that I was halfway up the driveway when I saw these two shadowy forms ahead of me. Dogs!

Visions of the dog's head and fangs flooded my brain as I recalled the one Dad had shot.

I stopped, but the shadows kept advancing slowly toward me. The hair on the back of my neck stood on end. My knees turned to water.

One of them slid past to the right and stopped behind me. Now I had one in front and one behind me. No place to run even if I could.

I shouted at the dog in front, "Get oota here, ye bugger!"

It gave a yelp and disappeared. I didn't even turn around to check on the other one. I just started walking in the direction of home, every second expecting to feel the weight of the dog on my back or feel its fangs in my neck. The suspense was so great that I wished it would just happen and be over with. Maybe the one ahead of me was waiting somewhere to ambush me.

Finally I saw the dull, welcome glow of light from the house and staggered inside, bolting the door behind me.

Not until daybreak did the nightmare visions disappear.

It was quite a few months after this that I spent my usual Saturday with the usual movies. One depicted an air force fighter pilot who had been demobilized and was now a drunken vagrant. While in the service, he had crash-landed on a remote island that somehow had not advanced in time. It had a hot, steamy climate and was full of marshland with all kinds of dinosaurs that were continually screeching and screaming throughout the whole movie. Continually drizzling rain added to the drama. The pilot finally did escape the island, but his present debauched condition was the result of the harrowing experience.

That Saturday night I had taken the bus home and was walking up the road. It was drizzling rain. I had just started walking when I heard this screeching. It was exactly the same as the sound the dinosaurs made in the movie. The darkness and drizzling rain made it all so real, and a swamp was only half a mile away, right by my house.

I knew I was not dreaming, because I was getting wet. Fear was with me all the way. The closer I got to the swamp, the louder the screeching.

Once inside the house, I turned up the light. Paraffin (kerosene) lamps were our only source of light. I could still hear the eerie sounds outside. I found a torch (flashlight) to take a look outside (without loosing my grip on the door handle), but could not come up with any explanation for the sounds coming from the marsh.

It was a few weeks later. I had come home from work. It was raining then, too, and there were the noises again, coming from the marsh.

Beyond the marsh lay the naval air force base where they practiced aircraft carrier takeoffs and landings, amongst other things. At this time there was a squadron of Neptune bombers there—big, bulky, clumsy-looking things with huge balloon tires. I could see them taxiing round the Perri track to where they would spin around, heading down the runway before taking off. The noises appeared to be coming from somewhere over there, but I still could not place them.

With daylight in my favor, today I was determined to get to the bottom of this puzzling situation. My father had a good pair of binoculars, so I asked him nicely if I could borrow them. Only after I had answered all the why and what-for questions and sat through a lengthy lecture on their care and safety, did he hand them over.

I took up a stand overlooking the marsh and focused in on the plane about to line up on the runway. As it started to spin around, the left wheel had the brake on while the two starboard engines came to full power.

There was the answer. The huge balloon tire on the wet tarmac gave off this screeching as the plane twisted round for takeoff.

A poor substitute for Tyrannosaurus Rex.

ENTERTAINMENT

The location of our home as the family of the gamekeeper was always fairly remote. The nearest neighbor was usually one or two miles away, but we were never lonely. With three sisters and three brothers at home evenings and weekends, there was always something happening.

During the summer months my father would be up and gone between four and five in the morning to check his traps and snares and remove any rabbits caught in them before the sun hit them; the meat spoils very quickly in the heat. He had to check his tackle three times daily during the long hot summer days, walking many miles in all kinds of weather.

My mother would be up shortly after Dad, get the fire cleaned out and started to boil the kettle for the tea, then make the porridge (oatmeal). It was poured into soup plates, sprinkled lightly with dry oatmeal (this was called "christening") and left to cool a little and set. She would then take out two large spoonfuls from the side of the plate and place them on top of the remainder, leaving a space that was filled with milk. After she had placed one at each setting on the table, she would shout, "Breakkkk ... Fast!"

Everyone would be there within two minutes. Any latecomer would be met with a scowl from Mam, which needed no words. My two older sisters, Cath and Lena, left for work on their bicycles after they had their breakfast.

My father was seldom present at this time. He would have his porridge when he returned from checking his tackle, which could be any time between eight and ten o'clock in the morning. My mother would join him with a cup of tea, listening to his news of what he had seen and done that morning.

Breakfast over, he would spend the rest of his day repairing or making new tackle, fixing his bicycle, working in the garden, checking the beehives (or someone else's beehives) or sitting in wait with the gun for the return of a hooded crow to its nest.

Dinner time was at midday, something light, usually a plate of soup or a piece of fish. The main meal, supper, was at night when everyone had returned from work and cleaned up. The roles were reversed on the weekend with dinner being a nice three-course meal—soup, followed by some kind of meat (rabbit, boiled beef from the soup, wood pigeon, or even a wild duck or goose). My mother made such a variety of puddings (sweets)—all kinds of pies, custards, steamed puddings, rice, pastries, and always the cup of tea to finish it off. This was also the time for lengthy conversations and the telling of stories.

Summer evenings would find us outside, weather permitting, sawing and splitting firewood. The logs were delivered to us by horse and pole wagon and dumped in a heap. From there it was up to us to get them onto the saw horse and cut these 10–12-feet-long by 18–20-inch-diameter logs into about 10-inch-long pieces with the two-man crosscut saw, and then split them into smaller pieces with the axe. It was usually decided at supper time what we would do that evening. It was not always firewood. My father might come in and say, "There is a good rise on the loch. I think I will go fishing for a wee while. Come on, Loon. You can row for me."

At that age I could never understand what caused the fish to "rise." One moment the loch could be like a mirror, not a ripple. One trout would break the surface (rise), then another, and another, sometimes hundreds of feet apart until, within minutes, the entire surface of the loch looked like a boiling pot.

The rise could end just as abruptly as it started. Amazing. What strange factor signaled the fish to start "lowpin" all at the same time?

It was many years after this when I found the not-so-magical answer. It appears that when the water temperature and other conditions are right, the eggs, or larva, of mosquitoes and other insects will hatch and float to the surface, causing a feeding frenzy amongst the fish.

In our absence Mam would take advantage of the time to do some baking. Oat cakes, scones, crumpets, rock buns and sometimes dough rings covered with a fine powdered sugar. My sisters might wash their hair or do some ironing for themselves. My mother would clean the fish that evening when everyone had gone to bed.

An evening excursion to the woods was always fun, all of us in a jovial mood, singing or whistling. The reason for the trip was to collect fallen tree branches to fire the wash house boiler for Monday's wash; it would be a waste of good wood to use the supplied firewood for the boiler. Dad would tie the branches in suitable bundles for each of us to carry across our backs for the journey home.

Sunday was not regarded as a workday, although Dad had to check his tackle just the same as any other day. My sisters and I always went to Sunday school in the morning, all dressed up in our best clothes and "Sunday shoes." Only once in a while would Mam and Dad attend church.

On Sunday afternoon, if the weather was nice, we would go for a walk around the loch, about three miles. It was always the same; my mother and father would walk well ahead of us, never in a hurry, arm in arm, followed by Cath and Lena talking in whispers and giggling from time to time. Mairi (pronounced Ma-re] and I would be running around looking for stuff, discovering stuff, and now and then approaching Mam and Dad for an answer or explanation of what the stuff we found was.

I recall one such Sunday afternoon when my two older sisters suggested they would rather take a bike ride than join us on the walk. Yes! Fine! "Awa ye go," says Dad.

We were almost back to our starting point when we saw Cath and Lena on the pier where we had started, waving their hands and gesturing with some urgency to come quickly. They had taken a ride to Lhanbryde, the nearest village, and bought two quart tubs of ice cream to share with us. They had laid out plates and spoons for everyone. What a delicacy! With the lack of refrigeration back then, ice cream was only available to us on very rare occasions.

You may have noticed that at this time I have not mentioned my three older brothers. The only time they joined us was when they were home on leave from the army.

It was never a chore or hardship to work in the garden in the evening. Everyone had their own ideas and input. We kids felt really useful, dumping weeds, fetching tools, or replenishing Dad's glass of water, which he called a "klie."

Come the winter evenings, our activities changed. With the onset of darkness around 3:30 p.m., outside activities came to a halt around then. Dad would be in his workshop making straw beehives, called "skeps"; if it was too cold, he would come in the house and take his accordion into the "end room" and practice the latest Scottish dance music tunes he had heard on the wireless until my mother called him for supper.

After the table was cleared with the help of the girls, my father would read the paper, with the occasional rude outburst containing his opinion of how certain situations were handled as well as a few adjectives describing the offenders—all of which usually fell on deaf ears. No response was expected anyway.

After the six o'clock news it was time for a game of cards. A choice of whist or pontoon was the option, pontoon being a variation of blackjack while whist was a very popular community game. We kids were never allowed to participate, but by looking over various shoulders I got a good grasp of this pontoon thing.

THE PEAT BOG

While living in the Glen of Rothes, where I met my owl (see "The Owl"), my father was not employed as a gamekeeper. He had applied for and gotten the job as gardener to Admiral Nasmith of Little Haugh. Dad enjoyed the change of work, loved gardening, and the fixed, eight-hour day with weekends off gave him time for his beekeeping and other hobbies. Our house, fuel and milk came with the job; the wage was about the same as he had earned as gamekeeper. The coal and firewood were never quite enough to last the month, but we could cut all the peat we needed from a bog on a farm that Nasmith owned.

That farm was located on top of the hills overlooking the whole Glen of Rothes—one of those views that, once seen, remains in your memory forever. The farm itself, however, was called Monny Mouies ("many small mouths") and it was the most godforsaken, barren, windswept place in Scotland. The tenant farmer raised mostly sheep, but had a few scraggly cows too.

One day, during a long hot spell, we stopped by on our way to the bog. Dad greeted the farmer with a hearty handshake and exchanged views on different subjects for a while. Just as he was leaving, he mentioned how little the cows had to eat because of the dry and sun-burnt condition of the grass. The farmer agreed, thought for a moment, and then exclaimed, "But look at the view they have!"

A special wheelbarrow and a peat spade are a must if you intend to harvest peat. No shops or stores carried them; to even inquire about them got you strange looks and glances.

No problem—Dad would simply make them. He had used them many times in his younger days, so he didn't need plans or one to copy; the images were stuck in his mind.

One Saturday morning I had accompanied Dad to the woods, where he selected a four-to-five-inch birch tree with a bend to it. He cut out a section about six feet long and carried it home. He and my mother split it from end to end using the big two-handed crosscut saw to make the two side rails. The top edges were flattened using a small hand axe, and one end of each piece was shaped into a handle. Three cross pieces were fastened in between them to form the base of the barrow about two feet wide.

The huge wheel, almost two feet in diameter and about five inches wide, came next. Two circles made from boards with backings nailed across them were spaced about five inches apart, then narrow pieces of wood were nailed to them all the way around the circumference of the wheel. The deck of the barrow got the same treatment, only this time the "slats" had a half-inch space between them. The wheel and axle went in between the side rails at the opposite end from the handles.

The spade was made of wood, also, except for the steel lug some three inches long and half that in width, which was fastened at right angles to the right side of it. The cutting edge of the spade was tapered in thickness to a fine edge.

Oh! The excitement when Dad announced the coming weekend would be spent in the peat bog.

Mam, Dad, my older sister Cath, my younger sister Mairi and myself were the crew. A large basket full of sandwiches, lemonade, tea, even a tablecloth, was loaded on the new barrow and off we set.

It was at least a two-mile hike to the peat bog. We took turns on the wheelbarrow, talking and singing all the way until we got there. We had a rest while Dad visualized the plan of attack.

The whole strategy of peat cutting begins with clearing an area of grass or, most often, heather. The first row of peat is cut by pushing the seven-inch-wide spade almost vertically into the ground, removing it, flipping the spade over, and pushing it in again about three inches ahead of the first cut—thus cutting sides, front and back—then lifting out the soggy lump of peat and laying it across the wheelbarrow. The rest of the row, usually about ten or twelve feet long, comes out more easily and is added to the barrow one behind the other, six or eight to the load.

The wheelbarrow is wheeled some distance away and leaned carefully on its side, allowing the fragile load to tip off intact. One row completed; back to the beginning.

A second row the width of the spade is cut, only this time there is no need to invert the spade after the first piece of peat is pulled from the ground. When the peat is freshly cut, each piece is about twelve inches long, seven inches wide and three inches thick. It takes very little effort to push the spade into the bog; in fact, you seldom need the assistance of your foot after the first row.

Come midday the girls would clear an area and lay out the tablecloth with all the food and drinks, then call everyone to come and eat. This was always a nice time for conversation, which seldom happened while we were working. It was a time to show cuts or bruises and complain about the hordes of mosquitoes that infested the bog. I have seen the back of my father's jacket glistening in the sun from the wings of mosquitoes on it.

Back to work for a few more hours before the long trek home. If we were coming back next day, we would just leave the wheelbarrow and spade. Even though there were other families cutting peat, there was little chance the tools would be stolen, and the same applied to the peat we had cut.

After a couple of weeks in the sun, the peat we had cut would be stiff enough to stack in "rickles"—a circular stack of six pieces, one end on the ground, the other ends touching like little tents. This would allow the air to pass through the stack and speed the drying process. There the peat would stay until the end of the summer. When my father thought we had dug enough peat, he would stay home, leaving the rickling, which might take a few more days, to the rest of us. By late summer the peat would be completely dried out, as hard as a rock, almost impossible to break by hand and now shrunk to a size eight-by-four-by-two.

My father would commandeer the farmer's son with the tractor and trailer to bring home the crop. This was a fine outing because he would let me ride in the trailer.

It was on one of these ventures, and we were all engaged in our various tasks at the bog, when we heard this loud cry. The figure of a man came staggering over the hill some quarter of a mile away, shouting and waving his arms. As he staggered, tripped, and crawled closer, his English accent became clearer—something about being lost for so long and so glad he had stumbled upon us.

As he sat there puffing and panting and gulping the water Mam had given him, Dad laid down his shovel and strolled over to him, inquiring, "Is there a reward out for anyone who finds ye?"

"Oh! I very much doubt it," was his reply.

"Well!" says my father, "Then I am afraid you are still lost."

HUNTER GATHERERS

Our lifestyles back in the early 'forties were very much different from the ones we have in today's world. We had very few possessions, but never considered ourselves as being poor. All working-class people were generally on the same income level, with the exception of some more highly skilled trades such as carpenters, plumbers, auto mechanics, etc. We all had to resort to the hunter-gatherer system to supplement our meager incomes.

One of my favorite foraging chores was berry picking. This was a necessity of life and gave us jam, pies and countless other desserts. These adventures usually took place during the week after I came home from school. My mother, father and sisters would meet me at the door armed with buckets, small baskets or cups, and off we went to some remote location never more than a mile from our house. Dad had found this particular spot while on his daily round of checking his rabbit traps or snares. The sooner we got there the better. Berries don't last long on the bush; if the birds don't get them, decay sets in quickly, and there is always the chance that some other foraging family will get there before we do. The Tinks (Gypsies) were the worst. They would roam far and wide picking every berry in sight and selling them to the local store.

When all our baskets were full, we headed for home, some of my sisters complaining about the scratches, Dad whistling the latest tune he was trying to master on his accordion, and Mam never stopping talking about the huge number of premium blackberries we had collected in the past two hours. She thanked Dad for finding the place and us kids for all our efforts, then she would go into a lengthy conversation with herself on who was entitled to get a jar of the jam or maybe a pie. I think I heard her mention the postie (mailman) and the doctor.

My father always planted a big garden. In addition to the usual vegetables—potatoes, carrots, lettuce, beets, etc.—he also had black currants, red currants, rhubarb, strawberries and gooseberries, which all contributed to the pies and jams. I can recall the time when my mother made this delicious rhubarb wine. When we asked her where she got the recipe she replied, "From *The Peoples' Friend*"—her favorite magazine.

Our garden was situated up by the dog kennels, the larder and a few other storage sheds. This became a problem when the army camp was set up nearby. When the berries began to ripen, it was a great temptation for the passing soldiers to help themselves to the bounty. My father found out this was happening and walked into headquarters, asking to see the commanding officer, who immediately greeted him with outstretched hand, "What can I do for you, George?"

The C.O. and my father had been doing favors for each other for quite some time so, after a couple of scotches and promises, they parted company. Next day at roll call and squadron parade, the C.O. announced that any personnel, regardless of rank, caught stealing from our garden would be severely dealt with. It is good to know people in high places.

In the autumn when the fruit trees gave up their harvest, we always managed to get our share of the bounty. Apples, pears, plums and cherries were acquired through good friends or, more likely, by barter.

Wild blueberries (we called them blaeberries) were also available, but one had to trek far into the hills to find them and they were much smaller than the ones in the stores today. Cranberries were also to be found in the same location, but they were also much smaller, as well as harder and very sour. We called them knowperts.

No trees grew on the hills, only heather, miles and miles of beautiful purple heather. However, in the small valleys between the hills there grew a profusion of hazel trees—more like big bushes than trees. Here again my father would alert us when the crop was ready for harvesting.

Since it was a good three-mile hike to the hazel tree valley, the trip usually fell on the weekend. Mam and the girls would prepare a nice picnic basket with sandwiches, lemonade, water, plates, glasses, and maybe a beer for Dad. The trip was always a good time to catch up with all the news and happenings of the week. My father never failed to come up with an interesting tale about someone or something he had encountered during his week. Mam would be kept busy answering questions from

Cath and Lena about cooking or baking, while my younger sister Mairi and I scurried around catching butterflies or bumblebees.

All of a sudden we were upon the valley. It dropped off so quickly it was not visible until you were really close by. It had very steep sloping sides, almost impossible to walk down. One had to slither most of the way to the bottom, to be met with a dense jungle of hazel trees. The ground was already littered with fallen nuts, which soon found their way into our baskets and were then transferred into the pillowcase Dad was in charge of. Any nuts remaining in the trees were shaken down by Dad, accompanied with the usual growling, puffing and panting. We gathered nuts until the supply dwindled and we had a good supply in the pillowcase.

We scrambled up the sloping valley walls to a flat area where the girls laid out the tablecloth and set out the food and drinks. By this time we were all ready for the refreshment; the long walk and hard work had raised quite an appetite in all of us. Rested and refreshed, we started the long trek home.

It was left to Mairi and me to crack open the nuts and collect the kernels in a big jar ready for our mother to use in her cooking recipes. That chore would be saved for some rainy day when we couldn't go outside to play. Mam would set us down at the table with bowls and hammers, where we would spend a fine afternoon cracking and chatting. She would keep us encouraged with a remark now and then on the wonderful job we were doing and the amount of time we were saving her.

Another foraging experience I enjoyed was the collection of crows' and seagulls' eggs. The crows' egg season came first. The team usually consisted of two of my friends and me. The "Crows Wood" was less than a mile from my house and consisted of no more than a couple of hundred tall Scotch pine trees, ten to fifteen inches in diameter with no branches for the first thirty feet. I was always delegated to do the climbing, armed with an eight-foot pole like a broom handle with a spoon bound to it on one end. I would have to spail (shimmy) up the trunk of the tree to a visible opening at the top. There were so many nests and they were so close together that they formed a huge platform on top of the trees. One was tempted to get up and walk around, but knew you could break through to disaster at any moment.

After I had hoisted myself through the opening and was safely seated on the structure, I could now use the pole with the spoon to scoop the eggs from the nests within my reach. I would collect eggs from nests with up to three eggs in them; four eggs would suggest they now had started to form embryos and would be no good for consumption. In order to get the eggs down to the ground, previous experiences ruled out putting them in my pocket, and to lower them in my handkerchief on a string was too time-consuming. We found the quickest and best way was to drop the eggs one at a time into my friends' hats held in their outstretched hands.

While I was up on top collecting the eggs, I would select the next best tree to climb and repeat the whole process over again until we got all the eggs we could safely reach. The average haul for the day would be around three dozen, and that was only about 10 percent of the number of eggs that were up there.

The hunt for seagulls' eggs was a whole different strategy. They nested high in the hills, sometimes a five-mile walk or more to their nesting grounds, which were not necessarily in the same place they were the previous year. These were what we called Salmon gulls, huge birds with black backs. Their eggs were much bigger than a large hen's egg, and they were delicious.

The Salmon gull puts very little effort into building its nest; it just scrapes away any stones or twigs within a ten-inch circle and lays her three or four eggs on the ground. The camouflage coloring of the eggshells and the lack of a visible nest makes them very hard to find. One had to scour the hillside back and forth in a very tight pattern. However, if you find one nest, you will have found a dozen or more since they are usually only about four to six feet apart.

There are seldom any gulls flying around overhead or sitting on their nests. Only when they have laid all their eggs and begin incubating them will they remain on the nest. The same principle applies here as did for the crows—nests with four eggs, let it be. I would collect as many eggs as I was able to carry on the journey home.

Many other people harvested gulls' eggs, so the location of a nesting ground was always a closely kept secret. I was always listening to the other kids in school when they would be making plans for their egg hunt the coming weekend, and I'd get there ahead of them.

My mother was always so happy when I returned with a huge basket full of eggs. Because of the severe wartime rationing, goods like eggs were in very short supply.

And so, foraging became a way of life. It may have spelled hardship to some, but as far as we were concerned it gave us food, enjoyment and entertainment.

THE U.F.O.

In the long evenings of summer, after I came home from work and had my supper, it was my delight to go fishing, surf-casting in the sea about a mile from our house. This stretch of beach was known as "The Bear's Head," named after the huge and only rock that protruded from the miles of flat sand. It was the cause of at least two shipwrecks over the years, their skeletal ribs still visible. I could see no resemblance between that rock and a bear's head; maybe there was at one time.

Every night would find me here if the tide was right—full tide, or a couple of hours either side of it. I would fish the two miles or so to the east and then fish all the way back. On the weekends, depending on the tide, I would fish right through the night. It never got really dark. I could always see well enough to tie a knot in the line, and by 3:30 a.m. the sun was starting to come up.

This particular night I was fishing my way back to where my bicycle was parked. The sea was like a millpond, not a breath of wind. The sun was shining, the tide was full—a perfect evening for fishing. I was casting from the top of the shingle (stones about four inches round) bank, which was about fifty yards wide and miles long. The sea had piled them up to a height of twenty feet or more over the centuries. Behind the shingle bank lay the same pine forest our house was in.

As I fished, step by step, a feeling came over me like I was being watched.

I looked around. Nothing.

I looked up and froze in my tracks. I was looking at something that I can only describe as a huge flying saucer, a U.F.O. It was all of two hundred feet in diameter with a raised center and tiny flashing lights around the edge. It was hovering about twenty feet above the pine trees, not more than two hundred yards ahead of me, and not a sound. As I watched in amazement, it started to creep ever so slowly from above the trees to over the shingle bank.

I had been watching this thing for at least five minutes (and I don't know how long it had been there before I noticed it) when it swept suddenly down over the shingle bank and out over the water, barely above the surface, disappearing in a split second.

There was never a sound, never a smell of spent fuel, and there was never a ripple on the water, which seemed very strange since it flew so fast right over the water and just inches above it.

I told everyone at home that night about what I had seen. They didn't show any signs of disbelief, nor did they ridicule me. The subject was never brought up again, and I never volunteered it.

It was many years after this that I had another strange encounter involving what appeared to be a U.F.O. My wife Ann and I had taken a trip back to Scotland from the United States, where we now live, to visit family and friends and see some of our old haunts. This particular day we were taking a road trip by car, driven by my older brother Dodd accompanied by his wife Crena.

It was a beautiful, sunny day, and this narrow west coast road provided us with some of the best scenery in the world. I had taken a lot of pictures and was searching for more. We had just crested a rise and were handed this magnificent picture of some highland loch—high mountains to the right and left, the loch itself stretching into infinity.

We slowed down to drink it all in when I noticed a strange object hovering some two or three hundred feet over the water, maybe a mile away. I called it to Dodd's attention, who agreed that there was something strange. With the car now stopped, we discussed what it could be.

My brother was much better versed in aircraft identification than I was, because of his military service, but neither of us could come up with a reasonable answer.

Ann and Crena all this time had been scanning the area of the loch and could not find the thing we saw. It was right *there*; one could not possibly miss it. There were very obvious rays of some kind emanating in a fan-shaped pattern from the craft to the surface of the water. Even with more precise directions, however, neither of the women could see it.

I managed to get two reasonably good photographs before it slowly disappeared. When the film was developed, it did show exactly what we had seen, even the rays—although they were not as vivid as on the day we had seen them. Our wives affirmed that if that object had been there like that, as it is in the pictures, they would have seen it.

One thing that might be worthy of further investigation—my brother and I are both totally color blind.

I still have the photographs.

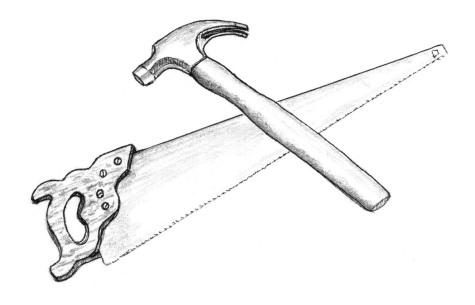

MY APPRENTICESHIP

In order to serve an apprenticeship, one must be at least sixteen years of age; that is why I spent over two years working as a woodsman before securing the job as apprentice carpenter and joiner with the firm Smith and Gordon, located at The Crofts of Dipple near Fochabers.

It was not much of a shop—a sprawling bunch of additions of various shapes and sizes attached to a rundown main shed with a corrugated steel roof. The only source of heat was a small pot-bellied stove on the back wall. There was no electric; we had one or two pump-up kerosene lanterns to give light, which was not unusual at that time. Everyone else had the same system. The outhouse—the Dry Dropper, the Lavender Shed—was behind all the other buildings.

Power to drive the various antiquated machines came from an equally antiquated, single-cylinder, kerosene-injector engine with two big flywheels, I think it was called a "hit and miss engine," whatever that means. It was connected to the main shaft, which ran the entire width of the workshop, by a long flat leather belt. The main shaft had various sizes of pulleys spaced throughout its length to serve the other machines by the same flat-belt system.

We apprentices were never allowed to use any of the machines except for the turning lathe, which was powered by a treadle. It could also be connected to the main shaft if the men chose to use it. There was also a big old mortising machine that did not require power—only muscle power, and lots of it.

There was another apprentice there by the name of George Hay, known as "Doddie." He was a year ahead of me and proved to be one of the best friends I ever had in my life. Even after we had served our apprenticeships together we still kept in touch throughout our National

Service, he in the air force and I in the army. After we were both demobilized we worked for a contractor in Elgin, one of the bigger towns in the northeast. After a few years, however, we went our separate ways but still kept in touch, even to this day.

Most of the work at the shop was done by hand; there were no power tools, not even an electric drill. Hand saws had to be kept sharp. It is hard to imagine in today's world, but we had to cut all the angle cuts on roof rafters and beams with handsaws back then.

The jack plane went everywhere with you. The steel hand plane usually stayed in the shop for finer work. The art of sharpening and setting them took months of practice. There were no toolboxes; a shallow boat-shaped canvas bag with two rope handles was used to hold your tools. A six-foot cord was wrapped tightly round it, making it resemble a big cigar. This was called a "tool bass." When going out on a job, it would be placed on the handlebars of your bicycle and held there with your thumbs.

We had to master every kind of job imaginable—chicken houses by the dozen, and the same number of trailers (called "bogies") for farm tractors. There were still a lot of horses used on the farms in those days, so there was always a demand for the big wooden wheels for carts and other conveyances. I think I could still make one today … with my eyes closed. Wheelbarrows and ladders were always a good standby when work was slow. They would be stockpiled in one of the back sheds awaiting a customer. Sometimes we would get a new house to build, which meant making every door, window, cabinet and staircase in the shop. There was no readymade stuff at that time.

The two partners, Alex Smith and George Gordon, were never happy with our work. It was either not good enough or we took too long. If we made a mistake, we were expected to work late or work through our whole lunch hour to fix it. Sometimes they would smack my ear for the least little thing, accompanied by a choice of words like "stupid," "useless," "good-for-nothing," "lazy," and the assurance that I would never be a carpenter and why should they bother even trying. Oh, well … only another four and a half years to go.

As the years passed they eased off on the abuse, but now and then there would be the occasional outburst, usually from Alex.

I had just finished my apprenticeship by one week and had received my first big paycheck. I was now known as a "journeyman." I was working in a new house in town. It was a Friday morning about 9:00 when Alex stormed in, obviously in one of his bad moods. "How many doors did you hang yesterday?" he shouted. I started to explain that I was working on my eighth one now. "That's no damned good!" he yelled. "You have to do eight a day if you expect to be paid the journeyman's wages."

I had taken five years of this kind of abuse. I had had enough. No more.

I laid down my hammer and looked him straight in the eye. "Could you be at the shop at five o' clock tonight?" I asked in as calm a voice as I could muster.

"What the hell for?" he shouted.

"I would like to pick up all my tools," I replied.

"What for?" he shouted, even louder.

"Because this is the last day I will be working for you," I said in a louder, stronger voice than he had ever heard from me before. I stood there right in front of him, not moving a muscle.

"All right," was all he said as he walked around me and out the door.

I kept on working and had no regrets about the decision I had just made.

Alex returned early that afternoon, smiling a fake smile. In a quiet, pleasant voice he said, "Hello, Ronnie, are you still in the same frame of mind you were in this morning?"

"Yes," I answered loudly, never lifting my eyes. I just kept on working.

In the same quiet voice he suggested that I gather my tools and, since it was Friday, he would take them over to the shop now. I told him I would see him at the shop as agreed and that I would finish my day's work as usual.

At this, he totally lost control and barked out, "Well! If that's the way you want it, that's the way you're gonna get it!" And he stomped out the door.

That was the last I ever saw of him. He was not at the shop that night, but Geordie Gordon was; they had obviously talked. Geordie expressed his disappointment at Alex's behavior, wished me luck, and assured me I would have no problem finding employment in the future.

It so happened this was not to be a problem. The following Monday I received a letter stating that I should report to the army barracks at Fort George, Inverness, to begin my two years compulsory National Service. It was the law then—anyone serving a five-year apprenticeship could apply for deferment; otherwise one would be drafted at the age of seventeen.

THE GREAT GALE

It was a Saturday morning in June of 1953, the day that went down in history as "The Great Gale." Never had such a wind storm been experienced by anyone in Scotland in living memory.

At that time I was staying in lodgings at the home of George Hay, the other apprentice who worked with me, in the town of Fochabers, only a couple of miles from the workshop where we were employed as carpenters. This saved me the ten-mile bicycle ride every day from home.

I can recall Mrs. Hay shouting to us to get up, adding that it was blowing a tempest. As we finished breakfast we watched all kinds of stuff go flying past the window. This was no ordinary wind.

We set off on our bicycles as usual, but had to give up. The wind was too much to cycle against. We walked, pushing our bicycles all the way to the workshop, thankful to have them to hang onto. Once inside the shop we thought we were safe, but the wind kept increasing in velocity. The corrugated iron roof started to lift; there was a mad dash for ropes and wire to secure it. We fought with it until we were exhausted and were thankful to get back inside.

George and I had been given the job of cleaning out the broken glass and putty from a bunch of old steel-sash windows, but it was hard to concentrate on work with the howling wind and all kinds of debris crashing into the workshop, which by now was collecting a crowd of stranded motorists.

Roads were blocked. Trees were down everywhere, and still the wind gained strength. An air of apprehension and fear showed on every face.

We watched as a large shed full of chickens belonging to the blacksmith next door was lifted up in the air, flown across the road and crashed down in the middle of the field, where it exploded in a cloud of splinters and chickens. It didn't stop there. The chickens were blown across the field until stopped by a sheep netting fence, which became a solid wall of chickens and shed parts some fifty yards long. Still, the increasing wind was too much for it. One end of the fence broke free and whipped across the field, releasing its contents then swinging back and forth in the air like a giant whip.

As we watched, a huge beech tree some forty inches in diameter had been blown over somewhere and was now going end over end through the field ahead of the wind. A fearsome sight. One could not believe the wind could have such force.

Just when we thought the wind had reached its peak, the roar became lower and louder. Work was abandoned for the day as all eyes were on the storm.

There was a small strip of woodland between the shop and the school containing close to a hundred or more good-sized trees; they had been blown over earlier and were blocking the road completely. With this extra surge of wind, the trees, one after the other, followed the path of the beech tree over the field and down into the valley by the river Spey until not one tree was left where the wood had been.

I was on one side of the bench looking out the back window; Dodd was on the other side, looking past me out the front one. By now the roar of the wind was deafening. The whole structure was shaking and rattling like it would disintegrate at any minute.

I caught a glimpse of a large flat object come hurling toward the back window. It was a large section of a shed wall. It missed the window, but hit the building with such force that it came through the wall, causing everything that was stacked there to come flying across the shop. I shouted to Dodd to look out, but my voice was swallowed by the roar. A piece of something hit him on the hand, enough to draw blood.

"I'm getting oot o' here," says he. "I'll tak ma chances outside rather than get killed in here."

And so the two of us set out on foot. A few people tried to persuade us to stay, saying it would be certain death if we went out in the storm.

We chose to take a route through the fields with the thought that we might be able to see objects coming toward us, giving us the chance to avoid them. We had not gone very far when we began to doubt our choice. It was nearly impossible to stand, and there was no way of turning round.

The wind at our backs, we moved forward in a crouch holding onto the fence, the wire cutting into our hands.

We had to stop every eight or ten feet. The wind was sucking the breath from our lungs, and breathing became more and more difficult. We were constantly looking out for airborne objects that were passing us by like rockets.

We finally made it to the valley with the river Spey at the bottom. The sloping bank to the river was a twisted, interwoven mess of trees, wire, even the odd car, but we found that if we just kept below the level of the field the wind was not quite so powerful. Thus, we struggled the last four hundred yards to the bridge over the river. We found a sheltered spot and rested for about ten minutes, not talking very much, before tackling the bridge, where we knew we would be once again exposed to the full fury of the wind.

We selected the bridge railing downwind. That way we would be blown against it and could perhaps pull ourselves along it. Well! It did work, but the force of the wind was unbelievable. Breathing was again a problem, and we both agreed later that, had that bridge been another twenty feet longer, neither of us would have made it.

As we entered the town we were a little more sheltered and could at least walk upright. Another fifteen minutes and we were home.

Doddie's mother greeted us with open arms, almost crying. She had been sure she would never see us again. We had a nice dinner, then told the whole story, each taking turns, to the rest of the family assembled there. We didn't need much rocking to put us to sleep that night.

Next morning, Sunday, was beautiful. Not a breath of wind or a cloud in the sky. I would normally have gone home midday Saturday, but this weekend was the exception.

After breakfast we set off on foot to retrieve our bicycles at the workshop. We took our time walking back, looking at all the devastation—roofs gone, trees gone, sheds and animal shelters missing, even fences blown over. Amazingly, the rickety old workshop was still standing.

I mounted my bicycle and headed for home, just taking my time on this beautiful Sunday to reflect on the horrors of yesterday and how really close to death I had been, and how two days so close together could be so far apart weather-wise.

THE DISTILLERIES

On being demobilized from military service, I had some difficulty finding suitable employment. Although I was now a fully-fledged carpenter, the labor exchange could only offer me the choice of two jobs in the whole of the British Isles.

I worked off and on at the potato harvest, grading and loading sacks of potatoes on trucks or railway wagons, until one Sunday my father was visited by Jack Cameron, a carpenter contractor from Elgin, a town some seven miles distant. They had known each other for many years, so visits between them were quite frequent.

During the course of the day, Cameron enquired as to where I was working. I explained my situation, and he said that he could use another good hand. He then turned to my father, as if ignoring me, and told him of two new contracts he had been accepted for, going into some detail on where they were and the type of work. They were both distillery jobs. He then turned to me and said, "Well! Throw your tool box in the boot and I will see you tomorrow at eight o'clock." Then he went back to the conversation in progress with my father.

Although he was related to our family through my eldest brother, it made no difference between him and me on the job. I did my job, and he left me alone, and I soon found myself in charge of two more carpenters and sometimes two apprentices also. We worked mainly on distilleries — sometimes on the huge warehouses, sometimes on the workers' houses or even the farm that was also owned by the distillery.

The distillery owners and all the employees were like one big family. It was difficult to get a job at a distillery. Jobs were usually kept in the family, the pay was reasonable, and the more important positions came with a house, fuel, milk and oatmeal—the same arrangement as the gamekeeper had with the Laird.

Three "drams" a day—morning, noon and five o'clock—were available to anyone who happened to be at the distillery at the time, whether a truck driver, a plumber, a carpenter, it didn't matter. Everyone filed past the brewer, who had a huge pitcher full of new, unaged whiskey and one glass.

You had no chance to add water, no time to sip it, and to think of transferring it to your own cup was out of the question. You had to down it in one shot. If you couldn't finish it, you just dumped the remainder on the ground. The three drams per day was the idea of the management. They thought that if they offered the three drams, there would be less chance of people stealing it.

This would be a good time to explain what is regarded as a "dram." Although a dram is an actual measure (one-eighth of a fluid ounce, just enough to wet your tongue), it is generally known as a glass of whiskey, the actual portion depending on the generosity of the supplier.

My father had his own rendition of the scale. It went something like this:

> 16 drams = 1 drunk
> 2 drunks = 1 fight
> 1 fight = 2 cops
> 2 cops = 1 judge
> 1 judge = 6 months

To be caught stealing whiskey meant immediate dismissal from the distillery, and by the time you got back to the workshop your boss would have already been informed of the situation. He would be obliged to fire you, or he would never be allowed to bid a job at that distillery again.

Sometimes temptation overruled common sense, and all kinds of devices were invented to get some of the liquid gold from the inside of the warehouse to the outside. Security was very strict. It was not only enforced by the management, but also by Customs and Excise, which had to have an officer present any time a warehouse was open.

The warehouses were huge concrete-block structures, hundreds of feet long with only one door. The whiskey barrels were stored horizontally, two or three high, on 4-x-4 cask rails. The only door had two padlocks, one for management and one for excise, so that one couldn't enter without the other. The inside of the lock had a short piece of glass tube behind the bolt, which could be broken with the convenient hammer hanging there in the event of someone being accidently locked inside. An eight-foot-by-eight-foot excise man's office, with glass on all three sides, was adjacent to the door on the inside.

One's only chance to get at some of the good, aged whiskey was when you were working in the warehouse, laying cask rails or perhaps building an extension to the warehouse. Even then, you were under the constant surveillance of the excise officer in the glass office.

My favorite gadget to get some whiskey was "the plumper." It consisted of a piece of 1½-inch copper pipe 14 to 18 inches long with a British penny soldered into one end and a tight-fitting cork in the other. The cork was attached to the tube by a short piece of leather bootlace. Another piece of bootlace about two feet long was also attached to the plumper, the free end having a loop to slip over a button. This whole assembly was slipped down the leg of my dungarees (bib and brace coveralls), and the loop on the bootlace slipped over the closure button there. It was almost undetectable and not uncomfortable to wear.

The operation of the plumper took some practice, having to be carried out in one deft movement, no fumbling or fussing.

The first time I used it was at the Tomatin distillery. We were putting the finishing touches to a big extension to one of the warehouses. The majority of the work was done through an opening in the outside concrete-block wall, until finally that access had to be closed up. The remaining work had to be completed through the main entrance, with the excise man there in his office. The work involved breaking through a new opening in the end of the existing building. The masons took care of that part while we carpenters busied ourselves removing the leftover materials. It was a long walk through the building with whatever we could carry.

On these trips back and forth I selected a barrel. Every time I passed it I would give the burlap around the bung a jerk until it came loose. I kept an eye on the excise man, watching my chance to use my plumper. It came on my next trip out; the manager arrived and went into the excise office with a handful of papers.

With their attention now on the papers, it was time for action. I stopped by the barrel as if resting, out came the bung, I pulled up the plumper from my leg, out came the cork, into the barrel, out of the barrel, jammed in the cork, and back inside the leg of my dungarees. A quick glance in the direction of the office assured me all was well. Yippee! I had done it.

I gained confidence the more times I used it, improving my strategy as I went—like touching every third or fourth barrel as I walked, as if out of habit, even when I knew the excise officer was watching; this would cover up getting the bung loose.

Getting caught never entered my mind. I was good.

One day I was coming out with a few boards on my shoulder. I stopped by my chosen barrel, stood the boards on end as if resting, went through the plumping routine like greased lightning, and was getting the boards back on my shoulder when I noticed the excise man heading for his office door then straight for me.

This was it. No more job, the wrath of Jack Cameron, not to mention my father (even if he was the main recipient of the spoils). My knees went all weak.

"Come with me, Sir," was all he said. "What for?" I asked. He assured me it was only a random check. Who did he think he was kidding! I dumped the boards off my shoulder and followed him into his office, where he told me he was going to pat me down—just routine.

He worked me over very thoroughly, apologized for any inconvenience he had caused, then opened the door for me and bid me good-day.

I headed back to where I had dumped the boards and picked them up. A quick check of his office assured me he was examining some paperwork, so I picked up my plumper, too, and slipped it back down my leg and went about my work.

A close shave. When I had dumped the boards, I had also released the leather bootlace loop from the button, allowing the plumper to slide down my leg onto the ground unnoticed.

NATIONAL SERVICE

I had just finished my five-year apprenticeship as a carpenter for which I had been granted a deferment from National Service in the British Forces until it was completed; otherwise I would have had to enlist at the age of seventeen. A few days after this, when I came home from work one evening, my mother handed me a letter. "That's for you," she said, and walked away with bowed head.

"On Her Majesty's Service" the envelope read. It was no surprise. The contents of the letter informed me to report to a location in Inverness, where I would be required to go through a variety of tests including academic, medical and psychological in order to grade my fitness for military service.

That day passed quickly—ushered from room to room, handfuls of papers, sometimes wearing very little clothes, even got to know some of the other draftees.

Another O.H.M.S. letter arrived within a week to let me know that I would be picked up at Inverness railway station at a certain time. I would be enlisted in the Seaforth Highlanders. Hey! I wanted to go in the air force!

We were picked up at the appointed time and day by a fleet of big military trucks. The attending officers and NCOs were quite nice to us, even referring to us as "Sir." We were whisked off to Fort George, which would be our home for the next eight weeks.

We passed through the gates of the garrison and drove onto the parade ground, where their attitude did a complete one-eighty. The tailgates of the trucks fell open with a bang; there was shouting, swearing and grabbing as they informed us we had two minutes to form up in three ranks (What is a rank? I wondered.)

We poured out of the trucks like a waterfall, stumbling, tripping while trying to hold onto our small bags or suitcases containing our worldly possessions, accompanied by the constant abuse and suggestions that our parents were not married. When we had formed up in three straggling lines, a sergeant called us to attention. This was accompanied with the promise that if anyone should move, he would personally make sure that person's mother would never recognize him again.

A few minutes passed before this impeccably dressed, stocky, mustached individual with a cane under his arm marched onto the parade ground, coming to halt at one end of the thirty-plus men. He made a smart right turn and began his stroll through the ranks examining every man with a gaze as cold as steel, and not a word. The examination completed, he marched smartly to the front of our parade, did a crisp one-eighty, and just stood gazing at us for a few seconds before bursting into a lengthy description of what he thought of us.

He had never in his whole career seen such a bunch of misfits. What had the world come too? What was he supposed to do with this bunch of delinquents, the dregs of humanity, unadulterated scum? He took off his hat and threw it on the ground, raving about how in his day if this was what the British Army was given to make soldiers out of, we would all be talking German or Japanese. He marched off, leaving his hat on the ground.

The sergeant added some more lengthy comments of his own before marching us off to our individual rooms and bed spaces, telling us we had ten minutes before assembling on the square to be marched to the mess hall for dinner.

There was very little conversation between us as we stashed our few belongings in our lockers and turned down our mattresses—a despondent group compared to the jovial bunch we were at the railroad station. As I sat on the edge of my bed, I took a little time to myself to reflect on the happenings of the past few hours, recalling the abuse of my apprenticeship. I thought nothing could be worse than that, but here I am, out of the frying pan into the fire.

The following week showed little improvement in conditions—the constant harassment, classes on how to do this and how to do that, rush here, rush there, haircuts and fitted out in our uniforms. By nightfall I was usually exhausted.

Our uniforms included various backpacks, belts, ammunition pouches, and gaiters that fitted over the boot and trouser leg to prevent any debris from entering our boots. The gaiters were made from a very stiff webbing material supported by an array of brass buckles, etc. Now, all this webbing, as it was called, had to be kept a uniform color, requiring the use of "Blanco," a shoe polish sort of material applied with water and a scrubbing brush. This was all very well for people who were not color blind, but I had known all my life that I, like my brothers, had this infliction. I could see no real difference between the parts I had done and the parts I had missed.

As we stood at attention by our beds the following morning, all our webbing laid out on our beds for inspection, the corporal in charge had little praise for anyone, but when he entered my bed space he exploded in a volley of abuse, accusing me of thinking he was some kind of moron who couldn't recognize the mess I had made. I tried to explain my color blindness, but he kept interrupting me with, "Report sick!" ... "Report sick!" ... "Report sick!"

The following morning I paid a visit to the medical room, as it was called, and explained my condition to the captain/doctor there. He queried me as to why this had not surfaced earlier. I explained that in my initial testing the staff spent very little time on my case; they were anxious to push everyone through as quickly as possible. He excused me of all duties until he further investigated my case.

I didn't have to wait long.

My name was up on orders to report to the medical room the following morning for an examination. The examination took several hours. Seven doctors, some of them civilian, put me through some rigorous tests—tracing dots in circles to form numbers, sometimes only a bent line. I heard exclamations of "amazing," "impossible," from the doctors as lenses were changed in the square eyeglasses they were provided with, as I traced out the number with the eraser end of a pencil.

The outcome of this whole episode was that I was no longer graded A1, which was the only acceptable grade for the infantry of the Seaforth Highlanders.

The following week I was before the company clerk to receive my documentation, travel warrants, transfer papers, etc., to Farnborough, England, where I would be enlisted in the Royal Engineers.

THE POTATO HARVEST

I n the early forties, during the war, all the schools closed for two weeks in October to allow the children to help with the potato harvest since all the men had been drafted to military service. We all looked forward to "The Tattie Holidays," as we called them. Not only could we make good money at this, we also got to meet other kids from different schools, which meant different girls too. Many a love affair was seeded and blossomed in the "Tattie Field."

The farmers would come to the school about a week prior to the holidays, state the number of help they needed, the number of days required, and the all-important rate per hour they were willing to pay. If you were interested in working for a particular farmer, you would raise your hand. He would then select the number of kids he needed, writing down the names of his chosen crew.

The selection was binding; you could not change your mind and go work for another farmer. It was a case of first-come, first-served, as far as the farmer was concerned. Some had the reputation of pushing workers too hard, some didn't like to pay enough, others didn't provide transportation, all of which helped you decide when to raise your hand.

Monday morning would find the chosen crew in the school playground, each one carrying his or her own bucket. The tractor and trailer (boggie) would arrive about 7.30 a.m. to transport us to the farm. It was usually a very cold ride.

On arrival at the field, those of us who were not already paired off would be paired off by the farmer. The "drills" that contained the potatoes ran the length of the field, maybe a hundred to two hundred yards long depending on the size of the farm. The length of the drill was divided into "stents," each about twenty-five yards long and marked with a four-foot-long stake—one pair of workers per stent. Anyone caught moving a stake was sent home there and then—on foot. The field so laid out was ready for action.

A second tractor with a contraption driven by the power take-off straddled the drill. A large spinning disk with fork-type things attached to it was lowered into the drill scattering rocks, dirt and potatoes over a six-foot-wide swath. As soon as the tractor and digger passed, we were behind it, picking up the potatoes and putting them into our buckets as fast as we could. When the pail was full it had to be emptied into one of the burlap sacks that were scattered throughout the length of the field for this purpose. The tractor continued on to the end of the drill, where it turned around and came back to the beginning where the whole process began all over again. By the time we got to the end of our stent and walked back to the beginning, the tractor and digger were already almost there.

And so it went for two solid hours with no rest. If the tractor had to wait until you finished your stent, you would have to face the humiliation of the other workers shouting at you. No one could hold up the tractor.

The two hours were followed by a ten-minute break when you would sit on your upturned bucket and eat your snack you had brought with you, never leaving your stent or joining any of the other workers, just thankful of the rest.

Another two hours of the grueling work. One hardly got time to straighten one's back before the digger was on their heels. Sometimes a few of the bigger boys would be offered the job of loading the full sacks of potatoes onto the boggie and unloading them either in a storage shed at the farm or, more often, taken to the end of the field where they were emptied into a shallow, prepared pit about a foot deep, three feet wide, and maybe twenty or thirty feet long. The crop was piled up to a peak about three feet high that would be covered later with straw and earth to protect it from frost until it was time for the potatoes to be graded for market.

Although this was hard work that required a strong back and the ability to lift a full sack of potatoes onto the boggie by oneself, it didn't have the monotony of the actual picking. If you didn't have enough empty sacks available for the pickers, they would overfill them or empty their pails beside them, leaving you to take care of it.

Lunch time (we called it dinner time) was twelve o'clock. The tractor and boggie would come up the field, picking everyone up on its way, to take us to the farm where we could get inside the hay barn to eat our lunch in some comfort out of the cold and wind. As was the custom then, we had a full hour to eat our lunch that we had brought from home. (The one-hour lunch time dates back to the era of the horse, which needed at least an hour's rest midday. It was consideration for the horse, and not so much for the workers.)

The aches and pains of the morning were soon forgotten after we had quickly finished our sandwiches and found that diving into the soft straw from the loft above, coupled with chasing the girls until they caught us, made short work of the one hour's rest we were supposed to have. Oh! The dreaded sound of that tractor being fired up to take us back to the torture of the tatties.

Another two hours without a let-up, round and round, up and down, no concept of time, and I would swear every new drill had more potatoes in it than the one previous. The sheer joy of silence when the tractor and digger shut down the engine at the beginning of the drill, signaling a ten-minute break. This time there was very little movement from any of the workers. Some lay there, stretched out on the ground. Some were rubbing their hands to try to restart circulation, and there was always someone constantly complaining about the condition of their feet.